CHAPTER 1

"*S*teady on!" Gemma Becker fastened the grip on her cane while tugging back her overexcited Cocker Tzu. Carefully, she pulled her suitcase and made her way up a gleaming cruise ship's gangplank while excited cruise-goers, seagulls, and ships reverberated around her.

Shielding her gaze from the mid-day sun, Gemma paused to marvel at the towering vessel before her. "It's as big as Buckingham Palace, Buddy!" she exclaimed, her neck arching to view the colossal smokestacks that pierced the sky and the multitudes of sparkling decks, each boasting an array of pools, dining establishments, and sun-drenched terraces. A sudden wind caught the American flag astern the ship, causing it to ripple gently against the backdrop of a clear blue sky.

She adjusted her wire-rimmed glasses as a blonde woman, pushing sixty, with a flamboyant feathered head-dress, teetered by with a dangerously sloshing martini in hand. Raucous laughter tumbled down from the deck above, mingling with the clink of glasses and the distant strum of a harp.

"Heaven help us," Gemma muttered under her breath. "I may have made a mistake for the first time in sixty-four years. The brochure promised a peaceful retirement aboard this behemoth."

After four decades as head housekeeper for London's posh Hotel LaFontaine, Gemma Becker had finally retired. Her tiny flat was closed up for the year, her favorite Earl Grey tea stowed in her bag, and her heart was in her throat.

If this first cruise doesn't work out, I can take the return trip home and call this infernal plan off, Gemma reminded herself. There's a reason I never bothered with vacations all these years. Goodness knows how many things could go wrong in one week, let alone one year: seasickness, falling overboard, running out of tea.

Bristling at the thought, she adjusted her pillbox hat and determinedly stepped forward.

"If I can make my way through London's finest hotel as long as I have, I can find my way on this floating one. It's time for us to retire in style, my boy. Goodness knows we've earned it."

Buddy barked excitedly as the ship blasted its horn. With a nod, Gemma leaned into her cane and crossed the threshold.

At the ship's entrance, Gemma spotted the first of the many American ship crew, including a handsome, uniformed man with salt-and-pepper hair greeting guests. "Welcome aboard the Princess of Paradise," he proclaimed in a jovial baritone. "I'm your captain, Scott Pierce."

Gemma offered a brisk nod, inching closer in line. She recoiled slightly as an exuberant blonde, her smile as bright as the sun, brandished an American flag mere inches from her nose. "Next stop, the Big Apple!" the woman chimed with a peppy lilt. "Peggy Swift, at your service – cruise director extraordinaire. Should you or your furry friend require any

MURDER SHE SANG

A GEMMA BECKER COZY CRUISE SHIP MYSTERY
BOOK ONE

HAZEL SMITH

For my Dad

May your ship ever sail towards the Morning Star.

Revelation 22:16-17

AUTHOR'S NOTE

I have a secret to share with you.

Most, if not all, of the Princess of Paradise staff, are inspired by family members on my father's side. Many aunts and uncles, cousins, and all my siblings have been baked into this cozy cake. Gemma's cozy cruise ship retirement adventures have only begun, so there will be more corners and characters to explore.

At the time of writing, my heart is tender as my dad bravely navigates the uncharted waters of cancer. Of course, he inspired Captain Pierce with his twinkling blue eyes, salt and pepper hair, and charming smile. Viv doesn't stand a chance when he's in uniform.

To my family: I brought you on board with the deepest affection and light-hearted humor. I hope you enjoy the reading as much as I enjoyed the writing.

A special note to Patty, my first Pet Cameo Contest winner: I only had plans for Buddy to be in one book. God planned for him to have a series.

xo Hazel

MURDER SHE SANG

A GEMMA BECKER CRUISE SHIP COZY MYSTERY

Book One

assistance, don't hesitate to reach out." Peggy reached down to pet Buddy, who waved his short tail furiously.

Buddy tugged his leash with gusto in his enthusiasm for more scratches, causing a nearby waiter to stagger perilously, a tower of champagne flutes teetering in his grip. As Gemma turned, a glamorous woman draped in fur swept by surrounded by a swarm of attendants. "Out of my way, morons!" she barked in a thick New York accent while a handsome but harried older man in a tailored suit shook his head beside her. "Valentina, please," he murmured. "Everyone is watching."

"Let them watch, Dirk!" She tossed her shoulder-length auburn hair, her dark eyes flashing. "I'm Valentina DeLuca, the greatest soprano since Callas. I should be the *only* head-liner on this floating shopping mall, but of course, you had to screw that up too!" Her harsh words sliced through the air, causing guests to turn their heads and whisper behind their hands. "Ugh, it stinks on here. What is that, fish?" She snapped her fingers at the pert blonde in oversized sunglasses behind her, who looked up from her phone for the first time since the outburst. "Piper, gimme my number nine," she commanded. Heaving a dramatic sigh, the young blonde clung to her phone as she dug around inside the large tote bag slung over her shoulder. Pulling out a small glass perfume bottle, she slapped it into Valentina's waiting hand.

Valentina doused her neck in a fragrant mist, the scent enveloping her like an invisible cloak. A self-satisfied smirk played on her lips as she returned the bottle to Piper with a dismissive flick of her wrist.

"Here we go again, Nina," Piper's voice was a low grum-ble, audible just enough for Gemma to catch as the group shuffled by. Beside Piper, Nina, a willowy figure with a cascade of brunette hair, clutched a folder so stuffed with sheet music it threatened to burst. Her response, though wordless, came through loud and clear—a swift nod, her dark eyes wide with a flicker of anxiety.

Gemma's brows arched in silent critique, her mouth a firm seam of disapproval, while the opera star and her entourage disappeared into the sea of boarding guests.

"I suppose it's a bit late to turn back now, my boy," she murmured as Buddy looked up at her quizzically. Gemma glanced at her luggage tag. "Hopefully, that shall be our last encounter with such a distasteful group of entertainers. I imagine I'll find much more joy in the quieter corners of the Princess of Paradise. Now, if we can reach the sixth deck, we'll find our private quarters and take a well-deserved nap. What do you say?"

Buddy wagged his tail affirmatively, and Gemma gripped her cane tightly. A touch of vertigo swept over her as she looked through the crowds for the elevator. The dizzy spell passed after a few bracing breaths. With a murmur of gratitude, she accepted a chilled towel from a steward as a trio of musicians tuned their instruments.

"Well, I could get used to this treatment. It's quite nice to be on the receiving end of customer service rather than the giving."

Gemma glanced over her shoulder, her gaze settling on the receding port of Southampton. Seagulls flew overhead and squawked as other boats bobbed on the deep blue waters below. A wistful smile tugged at her lips as a wave of fondness for her homeland washed over her. She would most certainly enjoy her retirement, even if it killed her.

* * *

A FEW MOMENTS LATER, Gemma clutched Buddy's leash more tightly as the bustle of the ship's grand foyer swirled around her. She squinted at the elegantly scripted room numbers on her key card, then at the corridors that branched off like veins in a leaf. "Now, Buddy, if we were back at the hotel," Gemma's voice trailed off with a hint of frustration, "I'd have had this mapped out in my head days ago."

Her faithful companion, unaware of the complexities of human navigation, responded with a cheerful wag of his tail and eagerly trotted along beside her.

She chose a hallway at random, the thick carpet muffling her sensible shoes. Each turn seemed to lead her further from her destination, the numbers dancing just out of logical order. Gemma's internal compass, honed by years of disciplined routine, spun out of control.

A young woman with dark curls, creamy coffee-colored skin, and a name tag that sparkled 'Meg Waters' bounded up to her, her chocolate eyes brimming with enthusiasm. "You seem a bit turned around. Can I help you find your cabin?"

Gemma studied Meg's open face and nodded, relieved yet reluctant to admit her predicament. "I'm looking for Cabin 6079. I seem to have taken a wrong turn twice or thrice."

"Of course! Follow me—it's actually on the other side of the ship." She extended a hand toward Gemma's luggage. "Here, let me."

Gemma followed the young woman as they wound through the ship's maze-like passageways. Meg led the way confidently, setting a pace that allowed the older woman to keep up comfortably.

Gemma's thoughts wandered as they navigated the labyrinthine corridors. Meg reminded her of the earnest young woman who'd replaced her at the LaFontaine. Ivy Stone's Midwestern grit and impeccable manners had always impressed her. The elderly matron wondered briefly how the hotel staff was faring without her watchful eye. Surely, Ivy was doing an impeccable job. After all, Gemma personally trained and approved her for the senior position. A postcard to the LaFontaine would appease her curiosity, she mused—a check-in on her cherished realm once she was settled into her new surroundings and sure of her plans.

Navigating the corridors, they passed under warm golden lighting that highlighted the ship's grandeur, a symphony of brass sconces and rich mahogany panels that adorned the walls. Each glance revealed more of the vessel's luxurious appointments.

"First time on a cruise, ma'am?" Meg asked over her shoulder.

Gemma held Buddy closer as they squeezed past a gaggle of tourists. "Yes, dear, and quite possibly the last if I can't even navigate to my quarters."

Meg chuckled. "Don't worry; everyone gets lost on their first day. It's like a rite of passage. I used to get all turned around when I started working the Princess, but now I know it like the back of my hand."

Gemma nodded absentmindedly as she strove to memorize the way to her room, determined not to ask for help twice.

When they arrived at Cabin 6079, Gemma's heart settled back into its usual rhythm. "Thank you kindly," she said as she pulled her key card out of her handbag.

"Anytime!" Meg glanced down at Buddy with a wink. "I hope you two enjoy your stay."

Meg's figure had vanished around the bend when Gemma swiped her the card, the door beeping in compliance. She allowed herself a wry smile. "Key cards," she muttered under her breath, her tone laced with familiarity and a hint of disdain. "I've dealt with more than I care to count. Spit spot," she called to Buddy, "let's try not to make getting lost a habit. In we go."

Buddy darted ahead, sniffing eagerly around their new space, his tail keeping time with their fresh beginning.

Gemma's fingertips grazed the wall, the smooth surface a tactile promise of the opulence surrounding her. A sigh, heavy with the weight of decades spent fluffing pillows and smoothing linens for the elite, escaped her lips.

As Buddy sniffed every corner of the cabin, she opened her suitcase. Gemma retrieved a modest cardboard box under a neatly folded stack of cardigans, its top graced with a single embossed "B." With deliberate tenderness, she opened the box and unfurled a soft cloth protecting a simple golden oval frame, revealing the black and white memory captured within—a young couple frozen in time. Her fingertips brushed lightly over the glass, lingering on the man's face with a softness in her eyes that betrayed her usual stoicism. She found the perfect spot on the bedside table and positioned the frame at such an angle that the first rays of morning light would kiss the faces within as her daily greeting.

With a nod of approval, she efficiently stowed the rest of their belongings: sensible clothes in drawers, a few toiletries lined on the bathroom shelf, and her crossword on the bedside table. Looking around the room carefully, she set her favorite mug, personal stash of Earl Grey tea, and digestives on the desk. Her nose wrinkled in distaste while she examined the assortment of complimentary coffees and herbal teas in the small basket beside the kettle. She flicked on the kettle and paused, captivated by the dwindling coastal cityscape visible through the rounded glass of the porthole, now a shrinking tableau, as the ship ventured forth. Soon, they would wend their way past the English Channel and enter the Atlantic for their week-long oceanic journey.

"Time to start our relaxing, carefree retirement life, Buddy! No time like the present. How about a cuppa?"

Stepping out of her shoes, Gemma padded over to the

armchair and scanned the cruise activities. Buddy's head rose and rested again, and his brown eyes tracked her.

The itinerary promised fitness classes, wine tastings, and classes on varied subjects. Gemma's finger halted at 'Opera on the Ocean.' Valentina DeLuca's name, emboldened and ornate, crowned the glossy program. As Gemma scrutinized the list of accolades beneath the renowned soprano's name, she discovered a litany of operatic triumphs that had dazzled audiences from Venice to Vienna. The diva's photograph commanded the page—a vision of intensity with piercing eyes and a posture that spoke of unyielding command. Beside the diva's listing, Lucia Rossi's name appeared: an alternate operatic talent scheduled to grace the stage on the intervening evenings. Gemma's lips tightened into a thin line, a skeptical eyebrow arching ever so slightly.

"I believe we have found the bee in Valentina's bonnet," murmured Gemma, her eyes narrowing. Buddy, meanwhile, circled three times, his tail wagging before he curled into a cozy ball. "A little competition can bring out the worst in people. They both have three nights each on this seven-day journey. Hopefully, they will be worth the hype."

Buddy's tail thumped in sync with his sighs. "You've got the right idea, my boy. How about a spot of reading before the evening begins?"

Gemma prepared a perfect cup of tea complimented by three biscuits on a plate, grabbed her dog-eared Father Brown mystery, and then settled back into the chair. Gemma leaned over her well-worn paperback, inhaling the comforting aroma of her freshly brewed tea, absorbing its familiar scent. She expertly flipped it open to the page book-marked by a farewell card from her beloved Hotel LaFontaine staff. After reading a few pages, her eyes began to droop, and she let the book fall open on her lap, relishing the silence that wrapped around her like a luxurious duvet.

Buddy was fast asleep, his tranquil breaths harmonizing with the soft, rhythmic water lapping against the ship's hull, creating a serene symphony that soothed Gemma's senses.

The serene hush abruptly fractured when a piercing scream sliced through the air from beyond the cabin walls.

CHAPTER 2

*G*emma's book tumbled to the floor, forgotten as the scream sliced through the muted hum of the ship. Buddy's ears perked up, his head tilting in concern. Gemma patted his head, her pulse quickening. "Come with me, boy," she murmured, her heart racing as she slipped on her walking shoes and steadied herself on her cane.

She stepped into the corridor, her sensible shoes silent on the plush carpet. The scream had come from nearby, and Gemma's keen sense of direction led her swiftly towards its source. Buddy seemed to sense the seriousness as he kept pace with his mistress.

Around a bend, she found Meg, the hospitality officer who'd been kind enough to guide her earlier. Now Meg slumped against a wall, her face buried in her hands, shoulders shaking with sobs.

"Meg, dear," Gemma called out gently as she approached. "Was that you who screamed? Whatever is the matter?"

Tears spilled afresh as Meg met Gemma's gaze, the smeared lines of black mascara mapping her distress. "Oh, yes, sorry, Mrs. Becker," she choked out, struggling to catch her breath amidst the tempest of her weeping. "I shouldn't trouble you with this. You're supposed to be enjoying your cruise, not helping me."

Gemma's hand found Meg's shoulder with an assured touch. "Nonsense, let's find somewhere to sit and have a chin-wag; you tell me all about it." She steered Meg to a nearby alcove furnished with a small bench under a decorative lifebuoy.

Settling onto the bench, Meg inhaled deeply. "I—I guess I got on Valentina DeLuca's wrong side," she said, pressing a crumpled tissue to her eyes. "I turned a corner too fast and walked right into her."

"Accidents happen, my dear. Even to the best of us."

"I know," Meg nodded, but another wave of tears threatened, "But she said the worst things about me, and, oh, she threatened to have me fired!"

"There are people in this world who beat others down to make themselves feel grander than they are," Gemma said softly but firmly. "I find it best to keep calm and carry on. They can only bother you as much as you let them."

A sniffle escaped Meg as she absorbed Gemma's words. "You're very kind to comfort me like this."

"Pish posh," Gemma said, her tone dismissive yet her touch reassuring as her hand rested firmly on Meg's back. "In all my years, I've witnessed more than enough tantrums over spilled tea and misplaced towels. Trust me, Valentina's outburst is small potatoes compared to some of the spectacles I've seen."

"Do you think I'll get fired?" Meg asked, fear creeping into her voice. "I worked so hard to get on the Princess. It's my favorite of the Royal Voyage Cruise Line ships because they let pets on board, and for other reasons that I can't really talk about."

Gemma cocked an eyebrow as Meg blushed and averted

her eyes from the older woman's keen gaze. "If they let go of someone as caring and diligent as you over one woman's tirade, they don't deserve you."

Buddy rested his chin on Meg's knee, and the corners of her mouth lifted as she stroked his sleek black and brown fur. "You're a cutie. How old is he?"

"Buddy is eight years old, yet still a puppy at heart," Gemma remarked, affectionately glancing at Buddy. "He's keeping me young with his energy and kisses."

"Thank you, both of you, for your kindness. I would love to stay, but I should return to work."

"Right," Gemma said, her gaze shifting to her simple silver wristwatch that clung modestly to her wrist. She rose to her feet with a steadiness that belied her age. "Carry on then, Meg. We've got a few days left aboard this ship, and I intend to make them memorable. I shall attend the opera tonight, if anything, to see if Ms. DeLuca's vocals outweigh the caliber of her character."

GEMMA STOOD before the full-length mirror in the quiet of her cabin, scrutinizing her reflection. The steel-gray strands, typically secured in a firm bun, cascaded gently around her wrinkled face and lent her gray eyes a softness that usually lay hidden behind her stern exterior. She smoothed down the fabric of her navy dress, its simple elegance accentuating her conservative taste. The dress fell just below her knees, and she paired it with a string of pearls that had belonged to her late mother. It was rare for Gemma to dress up, but tonight's opera dinner seemed an appropriate time to indulge.

"Floating shopping mall, indeed," Gemma scoffed as she

recalled Valentina's entrance. "The Princess of Paradise is a luxury liner if I ever saw one. I've seen plenty on the telly. Certainly, the price I paid was luxurious. We shall see if the meals and entertainment are up to snuff, won't we?"

She glanced at Buddy, who watched her from the bed with those soulful eyes that always seemed to understand more than a dog should. "Now, don't you start thinking we're going to make this a habit," she chided gently, the corners of her mouth lifting ever so slightly. She clipped on modest pearl earrings and gave herself a final once-over before deeming herself presentable.

"I've spent a lifetime in starched black and white uniforms. A single evening adorned in finery hardly renders me a pushover or pleasure-seeker. I will comport myself with dignity on this fine vessel, if anything, for the honor of my King and country. Come on then, tally ho."

Buddy's leash in hand, Gemma exited the cabin and glanced at the elegant signs to find her way to the Theater. The hum of anticipation buzzed through the corridors as other guests approached the soiree ahead.

Upon entering the opulent space, Gemma felt a twinge of discomfort. It was grander than any theater she had ever seen, with crystal chandeliers casting prismatic light across the room and gold accents glinting from every surface. Gemma's eyes swept across the room to the head table, where the captain, cruise director, and other distinguished staff members were arrayed in their finery, toasting with sparkling glasses. An attendant gestured politely, escorting her to a table where a group of passengers, already deep in animated discourse, paused to welcome her.

The maître d' guided her with a courteous nod to a seat beside a blonde woman whose plunging sequined teal dress rivaled the chandeliers' shimmering brilliance. "Well, hey there! Sit yourself down, honey. You're just in time for the show. Vivian Carlisle, but everyone calls me Viv." Her dyed hair shimmered under the lights like spun gold, and she extended a tanned hand covered in sparkling rings that revealed her age more than her face.

Gemma took the hand offered with a firm shake, trying not to wince at Viv's voluminous voice, which seemed capable of reaching even the furthest corners of the ship without aid. "Gemma Becker," Gemma replied, offering a polite smile. "I'm pleased to make your acquaintance."

"Oh, I just love your posh accent. I dated a gorgeous man from Manchester once, and he made everything sound good. But he didn't like dogs, so it would never last. Speaking of which, who's this handsome fella?" Viv cooed, leaning down to greet Buddy with an affectionate scratch behind his ears.

"This is Buddy," Gemma almost stuttered at the whirl-wind beside her that was Viv. Buddy's tail thumped against the plush carpeting as he regarded Viv with eager curiosity.

"Then you must meet my Fernando!" Viv squealed, picking up a shaking bundle of fur dressed in what appeared to be a miniature tuxedo complete with a bow tie. "He's my little protector. Watch out, though; he's the bad boy with a good heart type. Growls a bit."

Fernando glanced at Buddy with narrowed eyes before burrowing back into Viv's embrace, clearly unimpressed by the Spaniel's lolling tongue and panting ear-to-ear doggy grin.

As they settled in and perused their menus, Gemma was irritated and oddly fascinated by Viv's flamboyant presence. Every story she told to the other guests at the table was grander than the last, painting pictures of her past life on Las Vegas stages and standing ovations that seemed worlds away from Gemma's quiet life of service and routine.

Sipping on a martini, Viv swiveled toward Gemma, a

spark of mischief in her green eyes. She chuckled, the sound rich with experience, as she daintily plucked an hors d'oeuvre from the passing tray. "Oh honey," she said, her voice tinged with the promise of scandalous tales, "I'm counting on this cruise spicing things up a bit. I've sailed the seven seas on these floating palaces more times than I can count. I'm on the prowl now that I've shed my marital chains for the third time. I might snag someone to snuggle with when the nights get chilly—ring or no ring if you catch my drift." The treat disappeared behind her pink lipstick with an indulgent bite.

"So, what brings you on the Princess of Paradise? Love, adventure, running from the law?" Viv teased, her eyes glinting with mischief. Gemma caught mid-bite, sputtered as the sweet, tangy morsel of a goat cheese stuffed date threatened to go down the wrong pipe. "I say," Gemma managed to utter, regaining composure after a discreet cough to dislodge the treacherous date. "None of the above. I've retired at long last, and figured it was time for a holiday. I plan to travel on the Princess's various cruises, starting with this one. Buddy is my newly adopted companion and all the love I need in my life. If all goes well, we shall proceed with our plan; if not, we shall go home." She glanced down at her furry friend, whose tail wagged in response to the mention of his name.

"The Princess is fab for mature ladies like us who like to travel with our little furry friends. I've got all kinds of tips and tricks for traveling solo with a canine companion. We should meet up tomorrow and hang out with our cutie patooties. I'll make sure this cruise is a smashing success for both of you. Besides, Mr. Grouchy Pants could use a friend. Isn't that right?" Viv crooned lovingly at her Chihuahua, who returned her affections with a tiny lick of his caramel-colored snout.

"I—well, that's very kind of you to offer, but—" Gemma

began as dessert arrived—a chocolate confection that looked too beautiful to eat. Gemma caught Buddy giving Fernando a hopeful look, his tail wagging softly on the floor. The Chihuahua glanced back for just a moment before turning away haughtily.

Gemma's stomach churned as an operatic melody began weaving through the air from unseen speakers—signaling it was time for tonight's entertainment. The tables around them buzzed with excitement as guests readied themselves for what promised to be a lavish performance.

Was it the stuffed dates she ate or the irrepressible American next to her? Would she have to meet with Vivian 'Viv' Carlisle for a doggy date tomorrow, or was that simply a polite offer that meant nothing? Gemma doubted it. It would be poor manners to decline the invitation. However, it would be taxing on her nerves to accept. Helping a young service member such as Meg for a moment was one thing, but indulging the whims of an underdressed, over-made-up fellow retiree was quite another. What if she wanted to get together to chit-chat and mingle every day? Gemma sighed as she realized this cruise might not be as perfectly boring as she had planned.

Valentina, impeccably adorned in full makeup, stepped into the spotlight. She dominated the stage, her red sequined gown shimmering under the spotlight and red hair aflame under the stage lights. Draped elegantly around her creamy white neck, a silver necklace studded with diamonds clasped a single emerald that nestled into her plunging neckline, its verdant glint beckoning eyes to linger. Her soprano notes ascended majestically, resonating through the Theater and captivating the audience in their seats. Gemma couldn't help but be impressed by the singer's sheer presence. Behind her, the chorus girls provided a soft but firm foundation, their voices interwoven with Valentina's in an intricate tapestry of sound.

"That one," Viv said, nodding discreetly toward Valentina. "She's got pipes, but she's known for more than her high C's, if you catch my drift."

Gemma raised an eyebrow. This conversation was more interesting than chit-chatting about the weather. "Do tell."

Viv leaned back in her chair, her eyes never leaving the stage. "A few years ago, she performed on the Vegas strip at one of the places I used to headline. Valentina's has more scandals than a soap opera. Word is she's a real diva offstage, too. She thinks she owns every room she walks into, and everyone was put on God's green earth to serve her day and night."

From her seat, Gemma observed Valentina's every move, the diva's flamboyant arm sweeps and imperious posture holding the audience in a potent thrall. At her command, the chorus adjusted, their voices swelling in volume. Valentina's smile then unfurled, radiant as the spotlight that bathed her, soaking in the waves of applause with a performer's practiced grace.

Across the room, a tall man stood with his arms folded across his chest, his brow furrowed as he glowered at Valentina. Gemma noticed his jaw clench each time Valentina hit an exceptionally high note.

Viv followed Gemma's gaze. "That's her manager, Dirk Straggler. The word is those two have an on-again-off-again kind of thing. It looks like it might be off again for now." She chuckled and drained her martini.

Gemma noted a young woman half-hidden by the curtains in the wings, scrolling through her phone with disinterest that seemed out of place given the rapturous performance onstage. Her fingers flew across the screen even as Valentina hit her final, triumphant note.

"And then there's Piper, her so-called deeply devoted assistant," Viv added, clicking her tongue disapprovingly. "Might as well have a charger port installed at the base of her skull, the way she's locked to her phone. Kids these days, huh?"

Gemma nodded knowingly as the song reached its crescendo and then dwindled to a close. The audience erupted into applause. Yet amid the clapping and cheers, Gemma noticed how Valentina didn't acknowledge any of the chorus members or instrumentalists who had backed her so harmoniously for the performance.

Clad in a formal tuxedo, the ship sommelier made his rounds at their table, offering samples of wine for sipping, and halted to observe Valentina as she took her bows. His eyes shone with admiration, and he blurted, "I made tonight's special selection in honor of Madame Valentina. She is outdoing herself tonight. Isn't she *merveilleux*?"

"She certainly is...something, Henri," Gemma retorted dryly, noting the enthusiastic Frenchman's nametag.

Viv sputtered, wine threatening to go down the wrong pipe, and hastily covered her mouth with a glittery hand to stifle her laughter.

Henri advanced toward the stage, presenting Valentina with a taste from his selection, his eyes filled with adoration. Valentina contorted her features in disgust, dismissing him with a gesture and signaling her manager. Dirk acquiesced, his sigh evident amidst the clamor. Henri retreated, the sting of rejection etched starkly across his face.

"Love is blind," Viv scoffed with a twinkle of mischief in her eye. "Trust me, I've been down that road more than once. It's good that Henri is crazy about her, or else she might end with something other than wine in her glass."

Gemma nodded thoughtfully as her lips touched the chilled rim of her glass, the crisp Chardonnay a sharp contrast to the warmth of the evening. Viv's vivid tales of the crew and performers danced through the air, punctuated occasionally by her boisterous laugh. Overhead, a low rumble of thunder mingled with the festivities, a distant harbinger of a storm brewing beyond the ship's steady course.

CHAPTER 3

"Buddy," Gemma spoke softly in the early morning hours while she strolled through the vessel, stopping to rub the back of his ears. "Today, we shan't be drawn into any drama. It's a peaceful day, just you and me, and a spot of tea later."

Buddy's tail wagged in agreement, his nose twitching at the scents carried by the sea breeze. The sunrise unfurled a tapestry of soft yellow, blush pink, and baby blue across the sky. A tranquil symphony played as the waves kissed the ship's hull, the endless expanse of the Atlantic stretching around them, taking Gemma farther from home than she'd ever been.

The sound of frantic footsteps shattered their quietude. Gemma turned to see Meg Waters dashing toward them, her eyes brimming with tears.

"Mrs. Becker! Oh, please!" Meg gasped. "It's Ms. Deluca... Valentina... I was sent for her wake-up call, but she won't wake up!"

Buddy's ears twitched, registering the urgency in Meg's quivering tone.

"Lead on," Gemma urged, her voice firm.

Valentina's cabin door swung open to reveal an eerily silent space. The air was still; even Buddy seemed to tread more softly as they entered.

Meg lingered by the door, her hands clasped together in a tight knot of anxiety.

Valentina's shapely form stretched on her bed in the sheen of her silk nightgown, a chilling mimicry of peaceful slumber. Her leg, pale and still, hung over the edge of the mattress, the white sheets crumpled and pushed aside in a haphazard cascade. Motionless, her chest did not rise or fall, and her face bore a tranquility—the calm of eternity.

Gemma approached cautiously and felt for a pulse, her experienced fingers finding only cold, still skin where life's rhythm should have pulsed.

"Fetch the ship's doctor," Gemma instructed Meg without turning away from Valentina's lifeless form. "Buddy and I will ensure this room remains undisturbed."

Meg nodded and hurried off while Gemma looked around the room, hoping to find clues to the diva's demise.

Beside empty gift bags, a half-drunk bottle of wine stood on the nightstand, a tag dangling from its neck: 'From your biggest fan.' Next sat a glass stained with lipstick – Valentina's shade from last night's performance. Her eyes continued raking the room, noting the red sequined dress hanging among furs and designer pieces in the open closet. Gemma's brow furrowed, eyes catching on a fold-up cot behind the closet door. A second occupant in Valentina's quarters, perhaps? But why relegated to a cot instead of the plush double bed? Was Valentina anticipating company—a company she deemed unworthy of sharing her more luxurious accommodations? The plot thickened with each new question.

Her gaze shifted to the bathroom, where the door stood

ajar, revealing a bathmat askew, and towels that appeared hastily displaced. She stepped forward to peer into the gleaming white room, noting the recent use of the tub and hints of vanilla in the air. "Ugh," her nose wrinkled in distaste. "Did she add salts to her bath? Americans and their vanilla. That bean belongs in pastries, not all over one's body."

Returning to the main cabin, she detected another scent —faint but familiar. Inhaling deeply, she smiled as memories of her younger years in Northern England flashed in her mind momentarily: running her younger hands over verdant leaves and delicate purple blooms in the lavender her father planted in the garden. The peppery floral notes hovered like a ghost over Valentina's form and seemed almost out of place with their subtlety.

Did Valentina indulge in a late-night bath to unwind after her packed performance? Take off her makeup, attend to her ablutions, and retire alone in her room? No late-night carrying on in the casino or surrounded by adoring fans? All evidence pointed in that direction as Gemma glanced back at the woman's form lying in the bed. Her face was devoid of last night's heavy makeup, her glossy auburn hair smoothly brushed out, and her creamy pale skin was smooth as silk.

Gemma filed away these observations like a cleaning closet of assorted bottles and jars she'd cataloged for years as a head housekeeper.

The question now was, did Valentina's end come by her hand or another's? A heart attack? A drug overdose? Or perhaps something more nefarious, by her hand or another's? What secrets could the New York native have hidden that may have led to her demise?

Surely, it wasn't age. Gemma gazed at Valentina's ashen face, marred by only a few fine lines around her eyes and mouth. She hardly looked more than forty-five, even with devoted skin care regime revealed by the bottles of Estee Lauder and Coco Chanel on her bedside table.

Buddy sniffed quietly at the foot of the bed and nosed a small object out from under the white linen sheets. Leaning over, Gemma picked it up and turned over the small unmarked plastic jar with only a few streaks of white ointment left in the bottom. Furrowing her brow at the source of the mingled scents of vanilla and lavender, she set the jar back as Meg came back.

"The doctor is on his way. I notified security as well."

"Very good," Gemma said absently as she continued her inspection. "Keep guard so no one disturbs this space."

Meg nodded and took up a post outside the door, wringing her hands on her white apron as the two women waited for help.

What good they could do remained to be seen; Gemma shook her head as she looked at Valentina again. Last night was, in fact, her final performance of all time.

VALENTINA'S CABIN door swung open again a few moments later, admitting the ship's medical personnel. A man with quiet confidence and a weathered face that spoke of many years at sea entered, with a nurse by his side. The nurse's bright eyes and brisk manner contrasted sharply with their grim task. Buddy sat obediently at Gemma's feet, his nose twitching as new scents filled the room.

Dr. Jim offered a brief nod in Gemma's direction. "Morning, ma'am. I'm Dr. Jim, and this is my wife, Nurse Jo. I understand there has been an incident."

Gemma dipped her head slightly in acknowledgment, her

lips pressing into a thin line. She watched intently as they approached Valentina's still form.

Nurse Jo gently but efficiently checked for signs of life while Dr. Jim surveyed the room with an experienced eye. His fingers moved deftly over Valentina's wrist and neck, seeking the thrum of life.

"I'm afraid she's passed," Dr. Jim finally announced, his voice even but not without compassion. "Time of death appears to be sometime between midnight and three in the morning."

Gemma felt a chill at that confirmation, her mind racing through the implications. It was midnight to three when most of the ship slumbered as life slipped away from one of their own.

"Will you be able to determine the cause?"

Dr. Jim shook his head slightly as he rose from his crouched position by Valentina's bedside. "We'll need an autopsy for that. Nothing much I can do but keep her on ice until New York."

Gemma clasped her hands tightly before her, carefully considering the doctor's words before posing another question. "Would you hazard a guess? Natural causes? Perhaps something more intentional?"

Dr. Jim paused, locking eyes with Gemma for a moment. "Could be natural causes," he admitted with a measured tone. "But then again, it might not be." His gaze flickered briefly to the half-drunk bottle and glass on the nightstand before returning to Gemma's face. "It looks like she had a bit to drink after a bath, then went to bed, from what I can gather. As for what killed her, ship security will have to take over from here to answer that question. There's nothing more I can do here."

"Of course," Gemma quietly replied as she watched Dr. Jim and Nurse Jo confer.

The cabin door burst open moments later as a security team poured in. A tall, grizzled man with an impressive beer belly led the charge with all the subtlety of a bull in a china shop. His dark eyes swept over the scene before landing on Valentina's dead body with a mix of impatience and disdain. After speaking briefly with the doctor and nurse, he rested his hands on his leather belt, further straining the buttons of his white cotton shirt.

"Who are you?" he demanded, eyes narrowing as they settled on Gemma.

"Mrs. Gemma Becker, at your service," she replied, looking over her glasses at his sour face. "I assisted young Meg upon her request."

He grunted, scribbling something onto a notepad he had pulled from his pocket: "Michael Grimshaw, Chief of Ship Security. I'll get your statement, and then you can go."

Gemma blinked at him slowly over her glasses, took a deep breath through her nostrils, and drew herself up to her five-foot-six-inch. She recounted her observations methodically: the bath, lack of forced entry, the bottle with the note, Valentina's lipstick on the glass, and the pervasive scents in the air.

He looked at her as if she had grown another head. "Do you think the smell in here matters? From what I can see, Valentina DeLuca has a million perfumes and creams."

Gemma met his gaze squarely. "Three perfumes and six creams are visible to my count."

He snorted derisively. "Well, Mrs. Becker," he said, his tone making it clear he thought little of her input, "thank you for your report. You can leave this to the professionals. We don't need passengers playing detective."

As Grimshaw turned away to bark orders at his team, Gemma decided then and there that any further observations would be kept close to her chest. He might have authority on this ship, but she had decades of experience noticing details others overlooked. She doubted he would appreciate them and wasn't inclined to waste her insights on unreceptive ears.

"You can go back to your cruise now, ma'am," Grimshaw called out without turning around as he continued his investigation, "We'll take it from here."

With a measured exhale, Gemma crossed the threshold of Valentina's cabin, Buddy close at her heels. "Lord have mercy," she shivered in the morning breeze as she stepped beside Meg. "Valentina may have been a trying woman, but she had years ahead of her."

"I'm not sure who will miss her other than her fans, Mrs. Becker. She didn't seem to have many friends."

Gemma nodded sagely as footsteps and angry voices grew louder around the corner.

The corridor soon filled with the arrival of Dirk Straggler, his suit impeccable as always, and Piper Vanderhall, phone in hand, tapping away with a furrowed brow. Behind them trailed a clutch of chorus members, their faces etched with confusion.

"Valentina!" Dirk's voice sliced through the din, laced with annoyance. He strode forward, his irritation palpable. "Where the hell are you? The rehearsal started fifteen minutes ago. Piper and Nina have been calling you nonstop, and I've just about had it up to—"

Gemma put her hand out to stop him from entering the cabin. "Excuse me, sir, I'm afraid I have terrible news," she said, her voice unwavering despite the tumult within her. "Valentina won't be attending rehearsal today—or ever again."

"What are you talking about? Valentina! Don't think you can get away with this after what happened last night. Get your butt out here right now, or I'm gonna—"

Dirk attempted to push past Gemma just as Michael Grimshaw stepped out of Valentina's cabin.

"Mr. Straggler, Valentina is dead," the security chief declared. Dirk halted mid-step, the color draining from his face. "I need to ask you a few questions about your whereabouts last night."

A ripple of shock spread through the group. The chorus members' hands flew to their mouths, their gasps harmonizing in a dissonant chord of horror.

A silent sentinel amidst the growing chaos, Gemma's gaze moved swiftly to each face of Valentina's entourage.

Dirk shook his head, but his lips curled strangely, and his smile didn't reach his eyes.

With an air of nonchalance, Piper tossed her strawberry blonde hair back and shifted to catch the best light. Her phone, a seeming extension of her hand, angled to capture Valentina's door in the background. Striking a pouty kiss, Piper pressed her thumb with practiced ease and then smiled with satisfaction upon inspection of the photo.

Gemma recoiled at the sight. Did she take a photo of herself? What could Piper want with such a thing? Before she could ponder further, the chorus girls gathered around the tallest member, the willowy brunette Gemma vaguely remembered yesterday as they boarded the ship. What had Piper said to her during Valentina's dramatic entrance, 'Here we go again, Nina'?" Her staff were used to the demanding antics of the deceased diva. However, they wouldn't 'go' with Valentina ever again. Nina put a comforting arm around the chorus ladies beside her and pulled them in for a hug as they whispered among themselves.

Buddy tugged at his leash, pulling Gemma from her thoughts to the commotion. Crew members began gathering, and some guests stopped and snapped photos on their phones. "Word is traveling fast, Meg," Gemma remarked. "The good doctor is right. Valentina may have died of natural causes. Or not. And if she didn't, we are sailing nonstop to New York with a murderer."

CHAPTER 4

*G*emma made her way to the breakfast buffet, her mind replaying the morning's morbid discovery. She kept a steady hand on Buddy's leash, her eyes scanning the spread of morning fare with mild interest. A sudden voice, robust and confident, snapped her attention.

"Good morning!" The greeting rang out, warm and inviting. "Welcome to my domain, the heart of culinary delights. Jane Duffy at your service." The towering middle-aged woman with snow-white hair under her chef's hat beamed down at Gemma. "I've laid out a feast that will tantalize your taste buds. Please, enjoy." The chef's blue eyes sparkled as she gestured grandly toward the elegant array of dishes, her white uniform pristine against the backdrop of steaming platters, colorful fruit arrangements, and freshly baked pastries.

Gemma politely nodded, briefly meeting Jane's blue eyes. "Thank you, Chef Duffy. Everything looks splendid."

Jane smiled as she signaled to a dark-haired man with almond-shaped eyes in a crisp uniform. "Brent Li is our head waiter and will be at your service. We're mixing things up this morning, arranging seating to introduce fellow guests to one another. It's our little social experiment—think of it as a breakfast club with a gourmet twist." Her eyes twinkled as her hearty laugh rang out in the hall.

"Right this way, madam," Brent the head waiter murmured, his gentle baritone contrasting with the clinking of fine china. He guided Gemma with practiced ease, deftly weaving through the bustling dining hall to a secluded corner table draped in white linen. Gemma's heart sank as she spotted the familiar burst of color and heard the boisterous voice that could only belong to one person on board.

"There you are! I was hoping you'd come. Don't you think I forgot about our doggy date later," Viv announced, patting the seat beside her; Fernando perched on her other side in a comically small grey jogging suit, ignoring Buddy's friendly sniff.

"You remembered," Gemma forced a smile as she slid into her seat with an inward sigh, arranging Buddy comfortably by her feet. She observed Fernando's indifferent stance towards the ever-optimistic Buddy and suppressed a smile at the absurdity of it all. Brent materialized at their table with the stealth of a shadow, seamlessly transitioning to the role of attentive server.

"A mimosa, if you'd be so kind, sweetcheeks," Viv commanded with a playful wink that sent a rosy hue up Brent's face.

"Just hot water and lemon for me, please," Gemma requested as she rubbed her temples.

"Have you heard? Valentina DeLuca is dead!" Viv's voice rose above the hum of conversation as she leaned in conspiratorially. "Everyone is buzzing about it. She was found dead as a doorknob in her bed this morning. Now the big question is, was it an accident or murder? Can you believe it?"

Gemma cringed at Viv's overt delight in the tragedy. She fumbled in her purse for a tea bag, dunking it into hot water more forcefully than necessary. She grabbed a bran muffin from the tabletop basket and bit into it aggressively.

"Yes, I do believe it," Gemma intoned. "I had the pleasure of assisting the poor staff member who found her dead."

"Shut the door," Viv's hand paused, maraschino cherry halfway to her mouth. "You were there? What did you see? I bet your bottom dollar someone knocked her off because one thing is for sure: That girl had enemies. You have to tell me *everything*."

Reluctantly, Gemma began recounting the tale. As the story unfolded, she found the knot in her stomach unfurling with the release of the details in this strange turn of events. From the doctor's analysis and the wine bottle to Dirk's peculiar smile, Piper's impromptu photo, and the apparent grief of the chorus girls—the details flowed as Viv leaned in, nodding her head thoughtfully with each revelation. By the time she finished, Gemma felt a tangible weight lift off her shoulders. While Buddy's company was a comfort, his conversational skills were lacking. Viv, however, not only listened but engaged with an enthusiasm that was oddly soothing.

"Bravo, Gemma. Your attention to detail is top shelf," Viv exclaimed, her eyes sparkling with admiration and intrigue. "So, what's your take on this? A mere mishap? An act of nature? Or did someone give Valentina her final curtain call?"

"If I had to wager, I'd say it was intentional. There was no evidence of a natural death, nor that she took her own life. Could it have been an accident? Again, there was simply no evidence of that. Her room was practically pristine. She appears to have returned after the performance, undressed, bathed, and then performed her nightly routine before going to sleep. Only she never woke up, nor will she ever again."

Viv rubbed her hands together. "Ooh! A mystery to solve. No offense or anything, but this is a million times more exciting than bingo and shuffleboard. It's like those murder mystery dinners where everyone dresses up, someone dies, and then everyone else has to find out whodunnit. That means someone on board is the killer, and we could figure it out!"

Gemma's gaze settled on Viv, a blend of shock and awe coloring her expression. The notion of her first cruise—meant to celebrate years of diligent service—morphing into a murder mystery was beyond her wildest dreams. Indeed, the world of crime-solving was a far cry from the bingo halls and shuffleboard decks that were supposed to hallmark this retiree's leisure.

Yet here she was, contemplating a plunge into the depths of conjecture and suspicion like a seasoned detective.

Viv had barely finished her sentence when a shadow loomed over their table, the light dimming around them as if the sun had ducked behind a cloud. Michael Grimshaw loomed, arms folded across his ample midsection, his scowl so potent it could curdle cream on sight.

"I couldn't help but overhear your little conversation," Grimshaw began, his tone sharp enough to cleave the palpable tension in the air. "You two would do well to leave the investigation to our ship's professionals. Amateurs meddling in serious affairs can lead to complications."

"Oh, honey, if I had a dollar for every time a man told me what to do," Viv, unfazed by his stern warning, flashed him a grin as sharp as a knife. "Besides, I live for complications. It's what keeps my skin glowing." Her laugh was rich and unapologetic, echoing around the high ceilings of the dining hall.

Grimshaw's scowl deepened at Viv's snarky retort. "Don't say I didn't warn you." He pivoted sharply, every step away from them a rigid march, betraying his annoyance—or perhaps anger—for the cavalier dismissal.

Viv watched him go, shaking her head with mirthful disdain. "He walks like he's got a corn cob stuck where the sun doesn't shine," she muttered loud enough for Gemma to hear.

Gemma's laughter threatened to spill out, but she quickly stifled it with a napkin, pretending to cough to conceal her mirth.

Once Grimshaw was out of earshot, Viv turned back to Gemma with an expectant look. "So, what do you say, Gemma? Are you in? You and me, solving this mystery together?"

The question hung in the air like fog over the ocean—a challenge that beckoned with equal parts intrigue and risk. Gemma considered the offer carefully. Her practical nature recoiled at diving headlong into something beyond her usual expertise. She felt a flicker of excitement—this was her chance to step out of the shadows of her well-ordered life, to be the protagonist rather than a footnote. With Buddy as her trusty sidekick, she could almost envision them as characters in one of her beloved Father Brown mysteries, sniffing out clues and piecing together the truth. It was a chance to test her mettle, to see if her keen eye for detail could crack a case not confined to the pages of a novel or the walls of a fancy hotel.

Grimshaw's admonitions reverberated in Gemma's thoughts, a persistent rumble of distant thunder threatening her resolve. She paused, considering her next move with the care of a chess master contemplating a pivotal play.

"Perhaps we could discuss matters," Gemma offered with a nod more decisive than she felt. "It would be an academic project to keep our minds invigorated and well-ordered. We'll merely be observing and sharing notes."

Viv clapped her hands together with glee, nearly spilling her mimosa in the process. "Observing and sharing notes," she repeated with a playful twinkle in her eye. "Sure thing, hon. It will be our little project."

Buddy wagged his tail at their feet, oblivious to the weight of their conversation but sensing perhaps that excitement was in the air—or maybe it was just the scent of bacon wafting from a nearby table.

Gemma took another sip of her tea as Viv launched into a spirited discourse on potential suspects and motives—a tirade punctuated by emphatic gestures and bites of syrup-laden pancakes.

Watching Viv attack her breakfast with such gusto made Gemma self-conscious about her plate—bran muffin crumbs scattered like flotsam around Buddy's hopeful gaze. She eyed the pastry selection wistfully; it had been ages since she'd indulged in anything so decadent as a Danish or chocolate croissant.

She shook off the temptation with an inward scold; those sugary carbohydrates would kill her if she weren't careful. Besides, there were more pressing matters now—a real-life mystery.

"So," Gemma began after clearing her throat delicately, "we should probably start by piecing together what we know so far." She pulled out a small notepad from her purse—just one more habit from years of keeping meticulous records—and poised her pen above the blank page.

Viv leaned forward eagerly as Buddy snuggled closer under the table next to Fernando, who seemed to sense that his mistress was up to something meaningful—even if he didn't quite grasp what it was.

Together, at that corner table beneath an ornate chandelier casting soft light upon them both, Gemma and Viv embarked on their unexpected journey—one proper British retiree and one flamboyant former showgirl—each bringing their unique skills and perspectives to bear on a mystery that promised to be anything but boring.

CHAPTER 5

The clatter of silverware against china and the hum of breakfast conversation dwindled as Cruise Director Peggy Swift, with her ever-present smile, peeked her head into the dining room. Her voice, a bubbly melody against the drone of dining noises, broke through the space between Viv and Gemma.

"Ladies and gents, this is just a reminder that our fifty-five-plus water aerobics class with Katy will start on the top deck pool in thirty minutes. You don't want to miss out on the fun and fitness!"

Viv perked up, her eyes glinting with mischief as she turned to Gemma. "Ooh—after that breakfast, we should go. I gotta keep this heiny trim after those delicious pancakes. Who knows? Splashing around might shake loose some juicy tidbits about our little project."

Gemma frowned slightly at the thought of public exercise but couldn't deny a certain appeal in Viv's logic, especially with all the rich food and drinks on board. With a curt nod, she agreed to meet her at the class. After all, what was retirement for if one did not step out of one's comfort zone?

In her cabin, Gemma stood in a sensible navy blue one-piece swimsuit covered by a floral swim dress before the mirror. She pulled on her swim cap with careful hands, ensuring not a strand of gray peeked out. The swim cap clung tightly, tugging at her ears, evoking painful memories of past earaches from her few but frigid seaside trips long ago. At the tender age of thirteen, her chronic earaches damaged the deeper tissues of her inner ear, resulting in bouts of vertigo that had only worsened each decade. Only her esteemed employer, Sir Maximillian Hardy Humphrey, had been privy to the real reason for her use of a cane in the last few years of her employment.

"Right then," she said to Buddy, who was sprawled on the bed, eyes half-closed in relaxation. "No rest for the weary. I'm going to give this a go. A spot of exercise should do me some good." His tail thumped against the comforter as if he understood every word.

A giant yawn stretched into a lazy canine sigh as Gemma fiddled with her goggles, ensuring they were snug against her face. "Goodness gracious, it's been ages since I've donned a swimsuit." She cast a playful glance at her furry companion. "Aren't I adventurous, solving mysteries and swimming in public?"

Buddy's eyelids fluttered, a telltale sign of the inevitable nap overtaking him.

Gemma flashed a warm smile, deftly rolling a plush towel before slipping it into her tote bag. "You stay here, dear," she advised. "I'll brave the pool and the hurricane in high heels known as Viv. Who knows? Perhaps we might catch a clue while we're there."

* * *

GEMMA SHUFFLED onto the sun-drenched deck, the scent of chlorine mingling with salt air, and saw gray and white-haired retirees bobbing in the pool's turquoise waters. Viv stood out like a peacock at a pigeon party, her swimsuit a riot of color and daring cutouts that hugged her mature yet impressive figure. Gemma sighed, steeling herself for the encounter.

Viv's laughter rang out, as buoyant as the foam noodles that bobbed in the water. With her easy banter, she drew a court of silver-haired admirers, fluttering her unusually long lashes at a gentleman whose belly crested over his trunks like a friendly seal. Viv caught Gemma's gaze and waved her over with sunscreen-slick hands.

"Hiya honey, you're just in time for the fun," Viv called out, slathering another layer of sunscreen on her arms with a gusto that matched her personality.

Gemma hesitated at the pool's edge, self-conscious as she adjusted her swim cap. "I'm not sure 'fun' is quite the term I'd use for this," she said.

"Oh, please! You'll be splashing about like a mermaid in no time." Viv gave her a conspiratorial wink. "Besides, we've got our fox, Katie Fox, who is watching us."

A demi-goddess positioned herself by the water, her whistle poised for use. Clad in a striking fire engine red swimsuit, the sun glowed on her aviator glasses and golden locks neatly swept back in a ponytail. The buxom lifeguard exuded the timeless allure of a vintage pin-up—effortlessly turning the pool deck into her own retro photoshoot. From the shining eyes, admiring glances, and flexing pectorals from the male specimens in the pool area, the reason behind the sudden surge in male interest in today's water aerobics session was clear as day to Gemma.

Stowing her cane carefully on a pool chair with her tote

bag, Gemma descended into the water's cool embrace, gripping the bar tightly and moving with measured steps.

The chill of the pool sent a quiver through Gemma's solid frame, but she persisted, inching forward with care. The buoyancy of the water embraced her more securely, coaxing a gentle smile onto her lips.

"Alright, party people," Katie announced in a throaty voice, sliding nimbly from her lofty perch. The gathered men snapped upright at her signal, as attentive as soldiers awaiting a command. "Let's kick things off with a warm-up, then dive into the real fun."

Viv's banter flowed freely, her words punctuating the rhythmic splashing as everyone started to march in place.

"So, tell me about your life before this aquatic adventure," Viv said as she pumped her arms through the clear water.

Gemma huffed a breath, arms slicing through the water as she recounted decades spent within Hotel LaFontaine's opulent walls. "It was my kingdom in a way," she said between strokes. "Every crystal chandelier polished to perfection, every suite immaculate."

"Sounds like you ran a tight ship," Viv quipped.

"Indeed," Gemma agreed. "It wasn't just work—my life's dedication."

"And what about family?" Viv asked as they switched to leg kicks.

"I have no official family to speak of, really," Gemma shared. "I grew up in a small coastal town in Northern England. My parents were good, hard-working folk. Mam was a nurse, and Dad worked on the docks. I married my high school sweetheart at eighteen, but he died not long after. I went off to work in London and never really looked back."

Viv made a sympathetic expression and urged her to

continue. Flattered, Gemma was encouraged to share by her flamboyant friend's attentiveness.

Were they friends? Had they crossed the threshold from mere acquaintances? The whirlwind of events in only one day on board had warped time, making the hours bend. Indeed, they were only acquaintances, doggy date pals, and cohorts sharing observations of a mystery in progress.

This experience was a novelty, Gemma mused. She couldn't remember the last time someone had asked about her life story, much less about her inner thoughts and feelings. Granted, she'd never been one to engage in idle chatter during working hours, always deeming tasks at hand more pressing. Retirement had ushered in an era of leisure, starkly contrasting to the regimented days she once knew. Now, her most taxing decision was choosing between the decadent buffet or a specialty restaurant and whether to partake in an aqua fit or a stroll on deck.

As they moved into water jogging, Gemma's lungs strained for air; words fought against breathlessness. She vowed silently to resist cruise ship indulgences and embrace fitness with newfound resolve—inspired partly by Viv's vitality.

"The family I nannied for owned the esteemed Hotel LaFontaine, so when a position opened up for head housekeeper, they graciously offered it to me. The years flew by, and I met Buddy in my last months of service." Gemma's chest tightened at the mention of her loyal Cocker-Tzu waiting back in their cabin. "His former owner had an unfortunate accident. Adopting Buddy was a new chapter for both of us."

Gemma huffed for breath. "Now, I am here, and may collapse if I keep talking and jumping simultaneously."

"One death on this floating hotel is plenty, darling, so

don't overdo it," Viv quipped with a playful wag of her finger. "You gotta know your limits."

Their workout ended with cooling stretches that let Gemma's heartbeat settle into a less frantic rhythm. As they exited the pool, Peggy Swift hurried towards Katie, the cruise director's sun-kissed legs propelling her across the deck in her crisp white shorts. Her ordinarily cheerful features had given way to furrows of worry, her brows drawn tightly over eyes brimming with urgency.

Gemma's gaze followed Peggy's brisk approach, observing as she whispered intently into Katie's ear. The gravity of Peggy's words was immediate, and Katie's face dissolved into a severe and concerned frown.

Viv leaned closer to Gemma, curiosity lighting up her features like stage lights. "Something's up," she whispered.

Gemma nodded slightly and edged closer under the pretense of drying off with her towel.

"... can't believe it," Peggy said to Katie with palpable stress lacing the older woman's words. "Grimshaw thinks it might be murder..."

Katie's voice was barely audible, a mix of disbelief and concern. "And they think it was her?"

Peggy's eyes darted around before she leaned in, urgency in her whisper. "It doesn't look good at all."

Water trailed from their swimsuits, creating small puddles on the deck as they exchanged knowing glances and subtly moved within earshot, eager for more of Peggy's urgent whispers.

"Meg's in the hot seat now—hauled in for an interrogation. They're pegging her as a prime suspect!"

A cold realization gripped Gemma, sending a shiver down her spine as the gravity of the situation dawned on her.

"Meg? Who's Meg?" Viv whispered.

"A young hospitality staff member who had an unfortunate run-in with Valentina yesterday," Gemma replied. "She's the last person I would ever put on a suspect list. If Grimshaw has put her on his, we must clear her good name before her life is ruined."

CHAPTER 6

After Peggy's unexpected revelation, Gemma's mind was a whirlpool of thoughts. The mere idea that Meg, the gentle soul she'd comforted just a day before, could be responsible for such a heinous act was ludicrous. Gemma caught Viv's eye as the class dispersed, and the retirees shuffled off to their next activity.

"We need to clear Meg's name," Gemma stated firmly.

Viv nodded, her eyes ablaze with the thrill of the chase. "Any friend of yours is a friend of mine, hon. We'll crack this case wide open."

They agreed to reconvene after an hour to discuss their plan over lunch in the ship's dining room. Viv wagged a finger at Gemma as they parted ways: "Don't forget to wash off that pool water and slather on some moisturizer. I don't want you turning into a raisin on me!"

Gemma scoffed at the thought. Her skin had already witnessed sixty-four years of life; a few more wrinkles wouldn't change much. Still, itchy skin was an annoyance she could do without.

As she returned to her cabin, Gemma's legs were rubbery.

Years on her feet had given her stamina, but leg kicks were another matter entirely. Grateful for the steady support of her cane, she turned a corner and nearly collided with a figure that appeared out of nowhere.

"Oh, I'm so sorry," Meg wiped her eyes on her apron as she stepped aside to let the older woman pass.

"Meg, my dear," Gemma began with gentle concern, "I've heard the news."

Meg's eyes darted as if looking for an escape route before settling on Gemma's kind face. "It's awful, Mrs. Becker," she stammered, clutching her clipboard like a lifeline. "Mr. Grimshaw asked me a bunch of questions after you left and—"

Gemma looked at her tear-stained face and prodded her to continue.

"I told him about Valentina freaking out on me yesterday when I bumped into her, and then he started asking me questions. He—he wanted to know where I was late last night, and...and I can't say."

Gemma looked at her quizzically. "You can't say?"

"No, I can't," Meg's eyes filled with tears. "I would if I could, but I just can't. Not without—oh, I just can't, I'm sorry!"

"But surely you must have an explanation for your whereabouts?" Gemma prodded softly.

Meg bit her lip, eyes welling up again. "I'm sorry, Mrs. Becker...I can't say anything more." With that cryptic response, she hurried away down the corridor.

Gemma watched her go with a heavy heart. Meg's sweet mid-Western charm reminded her of her Ivy, the young lady who took over her position in London. What on earth was the young hospitality officer hiding? Did she understand what her reluctance to divulge her whereabouts could lead to? Her dream job on the Princess of Paradise might be the least of her losses if she refused to reveal the truth.

Gemma found it difficult to follow the signs back to her room as her mind whirled with the implications. She paused momentarily to lean against a wall as a touch of vertigo threatened to overtake her. Breathing rhythmically as her doctor advised, she counted to twenty and then opened her eyes. The dizzy surge subsided, and she leaned heavily onto her cane as she found her bearings.

Drat these dizzy spells that have plagued me for years, she gritted her teeth and breathed deeply in through her nose and out through her mouth. I hope they don't interfere with this cruise, much less the last years the good Lord grants me.

She retreated to her cabin, where Buddy greeted her with an excited yip and a twirl. Distracted, she peeled off the damp swimsuit and stepped into the shower, letting the warm water wash away the chlorine and salt. The steady stream calmed her nerves as she mulled over the situation with Meg. After drying off, she reached for her trusty bottle of unscented moisturizer and applied it liberally to reduce the raisin effect Viv warned her of.

Clad in fresh clothing—a soft pink blouse and comfortable tan slacks—she sat in her chair and patted her lap to invite Buddy for a cuddle.

"I'm quite certain Meg isn't our culprit," Gemma whispered, her voice barely audible above the hum of the ship's engine. She glanced around the vacant room, half-expecting an answer to emerge from the shadows. "But, what is there to do if she can't or won't clear her name?" She sighed, the weight of the mystery pressing down on her. "There's more to her story; I can feel it," she mused, her eyes narrowing. "Perhaps it's time to have another chat with that young lady and see if a touch of gentle persuasion might do the trick."

Distracted, Gemma sought solace in her Father Brown

book, allowing the detective priest's quiet logic to fill her thoughts instead of the chaos of suspicion and whispers that swirled around the ship. Yet even as she read, she found herself glancing at Buddy occasionally and muttering bits and pieces of ideas about what could have happened to Valentina.

Buddy merely cocked his head in response, his soulful eyes filled with unconditional support.

Setting aside Father Brown for a moment, Gemma picked up today's crossword puzzle from the ship's daily newsletter —a routine exercise that usually brought her satisfaction in its completion. Today, though, each clue seemed to remind her of their current mystery: 8 across—'Clandestine meeting,' 15 down—'Unspoken truth.'

Exhaling a deep breath, Gemma set the crossword down, and Buddy, sensing her disquiet, pressed his soft muzzle into her palm, offering silent solace.

The clock ticked away towards lunchtime as Gemma made one last attempt to focus on Father Brown's adventures —a necessary respite before diving back into their unfolding mystery. She resolved that by lunch's end with Viv, they would have a strategy mapped out that would absolve Meg and uncover who was behind Valentina's untimely demise.

THE SMALLER DINING room hummed with the low chatter of cruisers savoring their midday meals. Gemma navigated through the maze of white-linen tables, her cane tapping rhythmically against the plush carpet. She found Viv seated at a corner table, Fernando perched on her lap in a miniature sailor outfit matching her nautical-themed dress.

Gemma settled into the chair opposite Viv, carefully placing her napkin on her lap. Brent Li, their waiter, appeared with a flourish, and set down a basket of fresh bread rolls that wafted a heavenly scent toward Gemma. Her stomach growled in protest as she eyed the rolls but instead ordered a sensible salad.

"You've got more willpower than I do," Viv chuckled, selecting a buttery roll from the basket and tearing it open. "But I've always had a high metabolism, and dancing keeps me fit and limber."

Gemma glanced longingly at the rolls again before turning her attention to Viv. "Fernando has a more impressive array of outfits for this cruise than most passengers."

Viv laughed and picked up her toy Chihuahua to pepper his face with kisses. "He's the best thing to come from my last marriage. I wouldn't trade him for the world. Of course, he deserves to look chic with his gorgeous momma.

"Maybe if I had grandkids to spoil, I wouldn't doll him as much as I do, but it just wasn't in the cards, though I sure had fun trying."

Brent returned with sparkling glasses of water and salads. After taking their main course orders, Gemma leaned in toward Viv, "I spoke briefly with Meg after the swim class."

"Really?" Viv's interest piqued as she took a sip. "Well, spill the beans; I'm all ears."

"She was quite beside herself after Mr. Grimshaw plied her with questions."

"Mister Corn Cob?"

"The one and only."

"Other than his bad manners and equally bad breath, what's got her so shaken up?"

"She had an unfortunate mishap with Valentina just outside my room yesterday. Valentina threatened to have her fired. Upon questioning, Meg won't account for her whereabouts last night."

"What? Why?"

Gemma shrugged and sighed. "That's the mystery."

Viv leaned back in her chair. "The plot thickens."

"Meg popped up out of nowhere; it was rather unsettling," Gemma stabbed a cherry tomato with her fork.

"That doesn't surprise me," Viv said with a knowing look. "Staff here are like ghosts sometimes; they pop up and vanish before you can blink."

"What do you mean?"

Viv leaned in conspiratorially. "The M1, darling."

Gemma raised an eyebrow. "The M1?"

"The Motorway. It's a giant highway running the inner length of the ship. All the crew quarters and storage are located there, along with a maze of stairs that lets them access different parts of the ship unseen by guests like us."

"Goodness me," Gemma remarked.

"Yep," Viv continued, tucking into her salad. "You see those panels that look like part of the wall décor? They're one-way doors for crew members to slip through during off-hours."

Gemma processed this new information, picturing staff members flitting through hidden passages like phantoms in a Victorian mansion. She realized she had viewed the ship as akin to her hotel—transparent in its operations and accessible to all who walked its halls.

"Then I must consider every possibility," Gemma murmured, her mind drifting to the neatly stowed book on her bedside table.

Resting her fork beside her plate, Gemma exhaled a weary sigh, "It pains me to admit it, but with that kind of access and no alibi, we can't rule Meg out."

"That means we have our first suspect?"

Grimly, Gemma nodded. "We do, and it's the last person I wanted to put on the list."

CHAPTER 7

*G*emma's salad wilted on the plate, her fork tracing patterns through the arugula as she contemplated their first suspect. Meg's evasion tugged at her instincts like a loose thread begging to be pulled. Brent stopped at their table to check on them, then retreated to the bustling galley. The ladies nursed their drinks, the clink of ice against glass punctuating the silence.

"What would Father Brown do now?" Gemma mused aloud, her gaze falling on the bread rolls she resisted with a martyr's discipline.

"Father, who what now?" Viv arched an eyebrow, momentarily pausing her seafood indulgence.

"Father Brown. He's this fictional British priest in this marvelous series of books which—" Gemma started to explain.

Viv snorted, placing the shrimp back on her plate. "It sounds like he'd give you a sermon before solving any crime. He'd probably tell you to forgive and forget, eh?"

Gemma couldn't help but let out a half-smile despite herself. "Not quite. He had an uncanny ability to see into the hearts of men...and women," she corrected herself with a glance at Viv. "He would observe and understand human nature, examine the evidence, then unravel the mystery from there."

"Well, darling," Viv leaned in, her bracelets clinking together like chimes in a gentle breeze. "Let's do what this Father of yours would then: observe and list our suspects."

Gemma retrieved a small notepad from her purse and a pen that had seen better days but wrote with unfailing precision. She tapped the pen against the paper, signaling the beginning of their unofficial investigation.

"Let's start with those closest to Valentina," Gemma proposed as she wrote down the names in her neat handwriting.

"Dirk," Viv said without hesitation. "That manager of hers looked like he was two steps away from throwing her overboard during their last spat."

Scribbling swiftly, Gemma added Piper's name beneath Dirk's. "Piper," she stated, a hint of skepticism in her tone. "Valentina's assistant was rather dry-eyed today, more preoccupied with curating her online presence. She transformed a moment of mourning into a publicity opportunity, snapping pictures like a red carpet event."

Viv chuckled darkly. "The way things are these days—crocodile tears get likes and hearts."

Gemma's eyes narrowed as she pondered another potential suspect. "Then there's the person who gifted her that peculiar bottle of wine," she remarked, the pen pausing midair above the notepad. Her mind replayed the image of the sommelier, Henri, with his eyes practically sparkling whenever they met Valentina's. "A smitten soul could be driven to extremes."

Viv nodded slowly, her bracelets jingling in agreement.

"Henri, the wine steward. But would a scorned man go that far?"

"It's not unheard of for love to tip the scales toward madness," Gemma mused, her script continuing down the page. "Especially if rejection is in the mix."

Gemma pursed her lips thoughtfully before jotting down a question mark on her paper. The list was growing—a visual representation of potential malice aboard the ship.

Viv raised an eyebrow, a mischievous glint in her eye. "And let's not forget Meg. She's prancing from bow to stern, batting those innocent doe eyes at anyone who crosses her path. Yet, what if that sweet smile is merely a mask, cloaking a sly fox's cunning?"

"I'd hate to think it," she confessed, "but we must consider everyone." With a heavy heart, Gemma hesitated before her pen met the paper once again. She scribbled Meg's name at the bottom, the sound of the pen scratching against the notepad almost apologetic.

Gemma's pen rhythmically tapped against the lined paper, punctuating the silence with each deliberate strike. She leaned back, the furrow between her brows deepening as she contemplated the tangled web of relationships aboard the ship. "Who else," she pondered, a mere murmur overlaying the ship's gentle thrum, "might hold a grudge potent enough to wish Valentina's demise?"

"For all that she could sing, she had the personality of a piranha," Viv commented.

Gemma nodded. "From the moment she boarded to her final performance, she seemed to be making more enemies than fans. It's remarkable to think anyone who knew her in any capacity could be a fan unless one can overlook her manners and listen to her sing."

Viv raised an eyebrow, "Or ogle her assets."

Gemma's attention was diverted as a man approached the nearby tables with an uneasy shuffle.

"Isn't he the wine guy from last night's show? The one who was goo-goo for Valentina?" Viv asked.

Gemma's brow furrowed as she took in the sommelier's crisp uniform, once a second skin, hung on him like a costume he had hastily put on. She watched him weave between the diners, offering wine selections with a voice that lacked its characteristic lilt.

A couple at a nearby table whispered Valentina's name. Henri flinched as if the sound had physical form, his hand trembling enough to send ripples through the ruby liquid in the decanter he clutched.

His hands were unsteady when he arrived at Gemma and Vivian's table. The list of wines fell from his lips like marbles spilling across a hardwood floor—clumsy, loud, and out of place.

Vivian leaned forward, elbow on the table, chin resting on her hand, as she watched Henri with predatory interest. "Henri, darling," she purred, her voice laced with honeyed intrigue. "Are you okay?"

"Forgive me, *mesdames*," Henri exhaled, his words tinged with a sad flourish. "The world has tipped on its axis since the dreadful revelation." His eyes, brimming with an unspoken sorrow, searched theirs for a flicker of understanding.

"Would you describe yourself as, say, her biggest fan?" Gemma leaned in, her eyes glinting with a hint of curiosity.

The question broke whatever dam held back Henri's emotions. He pulled up a chair uninvited, his eyes gleaming with an unsettling fervor. "Madame DeLuca...oh, she was an angel," he sighed. "I watched all the performances I could catch online and in person. I knew all her songs by heart. She was everything."

He continued to speak of Valentina with the intensity of a summer storm. His confession poured forth: dreams of meeting her beyond the stage lights, of exchanging words that would bridge the chasm between idol and admirer.

His shoulders slumped, the weight of disappointment pressing down. "I worked so hard to prepare the perfect wine for Valentina last night," he lamented, a shadow crossing his face. "The perfect blend of rosé, her favorite. But she didn't even give me—it—a chance, not even a taste."

Gemma sipped her tea and observed Henri over the rim of her cup. "And last night," she interjected with a calm that belied her racing thoughts, "what did you do after the performance? Specifically, where were you between midnight and three?"

Henri's face bloomed red as a Bordeaux grape.

"In my room, of course," he stammered, tumbling out in disjointed fragments. "It—I—the regulations are clear, so I was in my room. I told the ship's security when they interviewed me. Where else would I be?"

He scrambled to his feet, his exit as stumbling as his confession, cheeks aflame. Gemma and Vivian shared a glance. With a mumbled apology, Henri grabbed his wine platter and hurried from the dining hall.

"You thinking what I'm thinking?" Viv pulled out a compact mirror and began applying a generous coat of bright pink lipstick.

Gemma nodded, her sharp eyes glinting behind her wire-rimmed spectacles as she reached into her purse. With a swift, practiced movement, she extracted the folded paper she had tucked away for safekeeping.

"Perhaps," she began, her voice steady despite the gravity of her words, "we've just met Valentina's 'biggest fan.'"

CHAPTER 8

*A*fter Henri's departure, lunch had dwindled to the last bites on Gemma's plate, and she listened half-heartedly as Viv, her voice bubbling with enthusiasm, rattled off the afternoon's itinerary. "Shuffleboard's next on the agenda," Viv beamed, her eyes alight with competitive fire. "Ever played?"

Gemma shook her head, her lips pursed in thought. "Can't say that I have. Strikes me as a rather peculiar pastime." Yet, a spark of curiosity flickered within her. After talks of suspects, the prospect of trying something new in this floating den of unknowns was oddly appealing.

"Well, there's a first time for everything," Viv winked. "I'll show you the ropes. It'll be a hoot!"

With reluctance belying her growing intrigue, Gemma agreed to join Viv for shuffleboard. As they parted ways, Gemma made for her room with Buddy trotting at her heels, his leash secure in her grasp.

The ship's corridors were a maze of understated luxury, each turn revealing more sumptuous carpet and gleaming brass than the last. In one such secluded corner, Gemma caught a glimpse of Meg in a subdued exchange with a striking man Gemma guessed to be in his early thirties. His curly hair framed his face in a carefree tousle, and his polo shirt hugged the contours of his muscular build.

Meg's usually bright demeanor was clouded with distress as the man held her arms with a firmness that bordered on urgency. He glanced furtively before leaning closer to whisper, "Don't worry. Everything will work out."

Gemma stilled, shrinking against the wall as doubt's shadow crept into her thoughts. She had seen enough of life to know appearances could deceive. He loosened his grip and hastened off, the swift motion presenting Gemma with a fleeting view of a gold name tag affixed to his lapel. Meg paused, tucked her dark curls behind her ear, took a steadying breath, and disappeared around the bend.

Buddy whined softly at his owner's sudden stillness, his head tilting in concern.

Gemma exhaled slowly, feeling the weight of suspicion settle upon her shoulders like an unwelcome mantle. Was Meg guilty? Was she involved in some sordid affair that led to Valentina DeLuca's untimely end? A chill ran through Gemma despite the mild temperature of the corridor.

"Meg wouldn't," Gemma muttered under her breath. "She couldn't."

Gemma's internal admonishment was swift. "She's no maid of yours from London that you'd trust with your life, much less your legacy. These are strangers you've only just encountered," she reminded herself, the recollection of her recent arrival on the cruise ship sharpening her self-reproach. "Looks can be deceiving."

Buddy nudged Gemma's hand with his nose, pulling her from contemplation. "Well, I know I know you, dear boy." She gave him a grateful pat before they continued returning to their cabin.

Once inside her room, Gemma sat on the edge of the bed and unclipped Buddy's leash. The dog settled onto his cushion with a contented sigh.

Gemma gazed at Buddy's trusting eyes and envied his simple world. There were no puzzles or crimes for him— only affection and the next mealtime.

"I thought retirement would be crossword puzzles and tea," she said aloud to Buddy as if he could offer sage advice. "Not this…whatever this is."

The conundrum lay before her: should she and Viv continue chasing shadows when guilt might already have been found? To clear an innocent person's name was noble; to aid a murderer was unforgivable.

"But *why* would Meg want Valentina dead?" she asked herself. "Surely, they only met on this ship."

One might wish another harm for many reasons: jealousy, money, revenge, love gone sour? But Meg? Gemma struggled to piece together a plausible motive that fit the young woman she had come to admire. Her mind wandered back to their conversation in the hallway only a day ago as Gemma comforted the distressed young woman who feared termination.

Meg's fear of losing her dream job was apparent. Was there more to it than that? What was she missing?

Buddy padded over and rested his chin on Gemma's knee. His soulful brown eyes seemed to offer solace and steadfastness amidst uncertainty.

"Alright then," Gemma decided after gazing into those eyes full of quiet support. "We'll figure this out somehow."

With newfound resolve but lingering doubts clouding her mind like fog over the sea, Gemma prepared herself for shuffleboard with Viv—perhaps another opportunity to observe the guests and glean insights into Valentina's demise.

She chose sensible attire for what she assumed would be

an afternoon spent amongst jovial retirees vying for victory on deck. Before leaving her room, she secured Buddy's leash and tucked away her list of suspects and Father Brown's wisdom within her handbag.

Emerging onto the upper deck, where rattan chairs surrounded glass-topped tables under sun umbrellas, Gemma blinked against the brilliance of daylight reflecting off the ocean's expanse, grateful for her oversized sunhat and prescription sunglasses.

There stood Viv beside a shuffleboard court marked by lines and numbers painted on its smooth surface; she waved energetically upon spotting Gemma approaching with Buddy in tow.

"Ahoy there!" Viv called out cheerfully across the din of excited chatter and clacking disks. "Are you ready to become a shuffleboard shark?"

Gemma mustered a smile for Viv's benefit as they exchanged greetings. "I'll settle for not making an utter fool of myself."

Viv laughed heartily—a sound so infectious even Buddy wagged his tail in rhythm with it—and took Gemma under her wing without further ado.

As they took turns sliding pucks along the slick court under Viv's tutelage, Gemma laughed despite her initial reservations. Shuffleboard was more straightforward than it appeared, and under Viv's boisterous guidance, it was even enjoyable.

The hours passed amid friendly competition and occasional doggy distractions as Fernando growled at passing seagulls from his perch atop one of the sun loungers, where he seemed to watch their game with disinterest.

Yet even as she immersed herself in this new diversion, part of Gemma stayed deep in contemplation, pondering

Meg's secret conversation and what dark truths might lurk beneath Valentina DeLuca's death.

* * *

THE CLATTER of shuffleboard disks echoed under the sun, each slide and collision a novel sound to Gemma's unaccustomed ears. Despite her initial skepticism, the game had proven to be a pleasant diversion that required a strategic eye she found satisfying to employ. She'd even managed a victorious round, much to Viv's delight.

As the game wound down, the players retreated to the comfort of rattan chairs beneath sun umbrellas, grateful for the shade. The horizon stretched out in a panorama of blues, the sea merging with the sky at a distant, hazy line. Palm trees swayed gently, their fronds whispering secrets to the breeze.

Peggy Swift moved among them like a honeyed sunbeam, offering water bottles and words of encouragement. "Remember, folks, hydration is key! You're all doing great out here with this sun and exercise."

Gemma twisted the cap off her bottle and took a long drink, feeling the cool water trickle down her throat. She watched Buddy approach Fernando with an eager wag of his tail, his eyes shining with canine camaraderie. Fernando's response was less than warm—a low growl rumbled from his tiny frame as he positioned himself protectively in front of Viv.

"Fernando," Viv scolded gently but firmly, "play nice."

Buddy cocked his head, seemingly perplexed by the rebuff but undeterred. He edged closer again, tail wagging like a metronome set to allegro.

Gemma chuckled at the spectacle before them—the two

dogs oddly mirroring their owners' dynamic with remarkable accuracy.

As Buddy made another friendly advance—this time greeted by a less hostile sniff from Fernando—Gemma turned to Viv.

"I saw something of interest on my way back earlier," she began in a low voice. "Meg was having what appeared to be a covert conversation with a man I have not yet met on board."

"Well spotted, Sherlock," Viv leaned in closer. "I want to hear everything."

"He was a good-looking man of about thirty, with curly, dirty blonde hair, I'd wager. He had a grip on her arms that seemed urgent," Gemma replied thoughtfully. "And he was assuring her that 'everything will work out.'"

Viv's eyebrows arched theatrically. "Everything could mean anything."

"Agreed," Gemma nodded slowly. "I'm not sure what to make of it yet."

Fernando finally allowed Buddy to sniff him without protest as Viv observed them with amusement.

"You think Meg's got herself tangled up in something less than legal?" Viv asked.

"It's difficult to say," Gemma said, twisting the water bottle in her hands. "She has yet to provide an alibi, and this rendezvous only adds to the mystery surrounding that young lass. It's looking quite dodgy, I'll grant you that."

Viv leaned back, casting a speculative gaze toward where Meg had stood earlier. "Well, we've got our work cut out for us then."

Gemma nodded in agreement as she watched Buddy finally settle beside Fernando without further incident.

"We need to talk to Meg," Gemma decided aloud. "But how can we get her to open up to two old women she met yesterday?"

"Hey, who are you calling old?"

"I beg your pardon," Gemma shot Viv a look. "For all your impressive form and physique, I'd wager it's been some time since your fiftieth birthday."

"Twelve years and two husbands," Viv winked. "And I'll take that compliment, Gemma. You're not so bad yourself for pushing, what, sixty-five?"

"Well, after water aerobics and shuffleboard, I feel my age. I do believe it's time for Buddy and me to rest properly."

"Someone beat you to it," Viv motioned with her chin.

Gemma's lips curled into a smile at the sight before her. Buddy lay belly up and basking in the warmth, his paws twitching gently in dream-chased bliss. Despite the tiny costumes, Fernando, ever the vigilant sentinel, remained atop Viv's lap, eyeing Buddy with a mix of curiosity and suspicion.

Viv's posture straightened, and her eyes widened as they fixed on a distant figure. "Is that who I think it is?"

CHAPTER 9

*V*iv shaded her eyes with a perfectly manicured hand.

"Look! Tell me that isn't the very woman we are looking for?"

Gemma sat up straighter and adjusted her hat as the midday sun blazoned down on them. Squinting against the sunlight glinting off the ocean's surface, she recognized Meg's wavy hair fluttering in the breeze. Viv jabbed Gemma in the ribs, almost spilling her water bottle.

"You've got that steadfast vibe going on, Gemma. Didn't you two have a bonding moment yesterday? Seriously, if anyone can gain her trust, it's you. I'd bet my last casino chip on it."

Blushing at the unexpected compliment, Gemma felt her courage and compassion swell.

"You've been given the gift of gab, Viv. Come with me; we can help this dear girl together."

"And crack this case wide open!" Viv declared, springing to her feet. She patted her hair into place and leveled a stern gaze at Fernando. "Stay put, mister. Momma will be back in a jiffy."

Leaving Fernando was a good idea, Gemma thought as Buddy trotted alongside Gemma, his leash slack as he matched her every step with a contented wag. He might put her off with a curl of his little lips.

The trio approached Meg cautiously, not wanting to startle her or seem too confrontational.

"Meg, dear," Gemma began, her voice a blend of concern and authority. "We need to talk."

Meg turned to them, her eyes brimming with fear and confusion. Her posture stiffened as if preparing to bolt.

"Please, hon," Viv added, "we're here to help you."

Meg hesitated, but the worry on her face spoke volumes of her internal struggle. "I…I can't," she murmured, looking down at the deck as if the answer might be scrawled there.

Gemma stepped closer, resting a hand on the young woman's shoulder. "Listen to me. If you don't provide an alibi for yourself, you could lose more than this job. Help us help you."

Tears welled up in Meg's eyes as she bit her lip, wrestling with the decision. Finally, with a heavy sigh, she spilled her secret into the salty air.

"Okay, it's tearing me apart, keeping this inside. But this has to stay between us; it's complicated," Meg confessed, her voice barely above a whisper. She took a deep breath, her eyes darting around nervously. "Last evening, I did something I knew I shouldn't have…and I didn't do it alone."

The glances that passed between Gemma and Viv were fraught with unease. Could it be that Meg was behind Valentina's untimely demise, and even more unsettling, that she hadn't acted alone?

"Late last night, when curfew was in effect, I was up here with someone special. We were just at the ship's prow," Meg continued, her voice barely above a whisper. "It was like that scene from the Titanic movie when Jack and Rose are at the ship's bow. It was just him and me, and the hours felt like minutes."

Gemma raised an eyebrow but said nothing, allowing Meg to continue unburdened by the interruption.

"Nothing happened between us," Meg blushed. "We talked about everything—our dreams, our fears... He gave me his coat when I got cold." She paused as if reliving the moment. "Before we parted ways, he kissed my cheek—a perfect gentleman—and walked me back to my quarters."

"Was this the gentleman I saw you with earlier, the one who assured you everything would be alright?"

"You saw us?" Meg gulped. "Yes, that's him. We've been friends for a while now. Well, maybe more than friends, but that's the problem."

"Sounds like a great problem to have," Viv intoned. "Unless he's a cheating no good piece of worm dirt like my first husband was. Then you should drop his sorry butt off the side of the ship. I'll help you."

Meg looked at the blonde woman with a mixture of awe and horror. "That won't be necessary, but thanks, I guess?"

"So, what's the problem?"

"Staff curfew is more of a suggestion than a strict rule. Staff fraternization, however, is non-negotiable. As long as I'm under contract with this cruise line, I can't date any other staff on any ship. If anyone found out what I was really up to last night, not only would I get fired, but so would Rob."

"Rob? You don't mean Rob "Ace' Cruz, that super cute blackjack dealer from the casino?"

Meg nodded glumly as Viv's brow furrowed. Gemma glanced at her companion and made a mental note to ask her about it later.

"But why protect him at your own risk?" Gemma prodded.

Meg looked at them both with earnest eyes. "Because he doesn't deserve to lose his job over this." Her voice cracked as she added, "I'm not worried about myself. It's my dream job, and I worked so hard to get here and everything, but I'd hate myself if he lost his job over this. I should tell Mr. Grimshaw the truth, but I can't. I don't know *what* to do."

The air around them seemed charged with Meg's anxiety and determination; it was palpable and raw.

"Thank you for telling us the truth," Gemma patted Meg on the arm. "Your secret is safe with us."

Her sharp gaze met Viv's, her eyes brimming with an unspoken query of their next move while Meg dabbed at her moistening eyes.

"I—I have to get back to work," Meg nodded gratefully and excused herself, hurrying away as if fleeing from her confession.

As she vanished from sight, Gemma felt the weight of what they had uncovered settle on her shoulders. The mystery had deepened, taking on new and delicate shades.

"You were right, Viv," Gemma blew out a breath, "That was a productive conversation. Only now, we can do nothing to help a woman who won't help herself."

Viv's solemn nod mirrored Gemma's resolve as she pivoted from the ship's railing, her gaze sweeping over the vast, undulating expanse of blue. Gemma's thoughts swirled, abuzz with revelations, as worry for the staff member weighed down her heart—a young woman tangled in a web of secrets and unyielding regulations.

* * *

FERNANDO'S EARS TWITCHED, his tiny frame tense as he caught the familiar scent of his mistress Viv weaving through the sea air. The minute she approached, he launched into joyful yapping, circling her feet like a satellite orbiting its planet. Viv scooped him up, nestling him in the crook of her arm, his bejeweled collar sparkling in the sunlight.

"Darling Fernando, my little guardian angel," she cooed, adjusting his miniature sailor hat. "You make a girl feel so safe."

Gemma observed the pair with a hint of amusement. The sight of Fernando decked out in his sailor suit was an unexpected balm to her roiling thoughts.

Viv caught Gemma's eye, a knowing glint in hers. "Rob's a good fella, Gemma. He's worked many casino tables while I fluttered around these Princess cruises. He wouldn't harm a fly."

Gemma sighed and nodded, watching the wake churn behind the ship. The truth about Meg and Rob could clear Meg's name but would fling them both into troubled waters with the ship's strict fraternization policy.

"Viv," Gemma started, adjusting her glasses with her finger. "We're sitting on information that could exonerate Meg. But if we honor her request to stay silent…"

Vivian thoughtfully tapped her painted fingernail against her lips before leaning closer to Gemma. "I get it. Meet me for dinner tonight. I've got a plan cooking that'll do more than simmer the pot."

With that cryptic promise dangling between them like a baited hook, Viv turned on her heel—Fernando cradled in her arms—and strutted away, leaving Gemma to ponder what evening tides would bring.

CHAPTER 10

Gemma's hand froze mid-stroke as she brushed Buddy's silky coat. An urgent rap on her cabin door interrupted the rhythmic sound of the brush against fur. She glanced at the clock. Dinner wasn't for another hour, yet there was Viv, peering in through the doorway, her eyes glinting with mischief.

"Sorry for springing this on you, Gemma," Viv called out, her tone laced with a breathless urgency that cut through the room's calm. "We gotta go right now."

"Go? Where? Why?"

Viv winked. "Just trust me, honey. Grab your stuff. We're on a tight schedule."

Curiosity nipped at Gemma's heels as she caught up with Viv, who had paused at an elevator door. As they ascended to the upper deck, Gemma gripped her cane more tightly and tried to steady her breathing, hoping her vertigo wouldn't choose this moment to make an appearance. The last thing she wanted was to tell the vibrant woman who had befriended her, like it or not, how old she felt sometimes. Sixty was supposed to be the new fifty, she had read in a

Hello magazine a guest had left in a hotel room during her last weeks of work. Gemma sighed wistfully, aspiring for that inspirational saying to prove true as she quickened her pace.

Barely had Gemma reached the bridge entrance when the sun's fading brilliance brushed the horizon, a fleeting spectacle gone too soon for her appreciation. Viv pressed her brightly manicured fingers against the glass door, a sly smile on her lips. Inside, a junior bridge staff member caught sight of them.

"Teddy!" Viv called lightly and flashed the officer a dazzling smile. Gemma raised an eyebrow as Teddy returned the smile, a blush creeping up his neck. He spoke into a handset and then gestured toward them with a nod. Moments later, Captain Scott Pierce emerged from the bridge's inner sanctum. Dressed immaculately in his crisp white uniform adorned with gold braids and a commanding captain's hat that accentuated his distinguished hair, his piercing blue gaze swept over the pair, finally resting on Viv with a warm recognition.

"Vivian Carlisle," he greeted, the corners of his mouth lifting ever so slightly. "Always a delight to see you. Might I inquire as to the occasion? And, if I may, your esteemed companion?"

Viv beamed and rested her hand lightly on his arm. "Captain Pierce, it's my delight to introduce you to one of London's finest, Mrs. Gemma Becker."

The captain greeted Gemma with a warm smile. "I recall meeting you yesterday, just before Ms. DeLuca made her memorable entrance."

"Memorable indeed," Gemma shook his large hand in greeting. "Pleasure to make your acquaintance again, Sir. As to the occasion for our impromptu visit for such a busy man—"

Gemma's eyes flickered to Viv, who was utterly trans-fixed, her gaze locked on Captain Pierce, open admiration etched across her features as she looked up at him, utterly captivated.

She gave her besotted companion a hard nudge in the ribs, silently pleading with her to explain what on God's green earth and bright blue sea could be the reason for pulling the highest-ranking member of the ship from his duties.

Viv snapped back to the present and edged forward, leaning in closer than was strictly necessary. "Captain Pierce," she cooed, "I just wanted to praise one of your delightful crew members personally."

Gemma's brow furrowed in puzzlement as she watched Viv effortlessly continue. "Meg Waters is an absolute gem. My insomnia was rearing its ugly head again last night, not a wink of sleep—and there she was, a vision in her hospitality uniform, like an angel in the dead of night."

The captain listened attentively as Viv continued.

"Meg was a perfect companion, never leaving my side, though I kept her up long past the recommended staff curfew. She walked and talked with me until I felt sleep coming over me. It must have been nearly three in the morning when she dropped me off at my cabin. She would have tucked me in, too, if I hadn't insisted she grab a few winks before her shift. Give that girl a raise, would you? She's a peach," Viv finished with an appreciative sigh.

What the Dickens was Viv up to? Gemma held her breath, knowing that Meg had been elsewhere then—but the captain seemed none the wiser.

"I'll make a point of highlighting Meg's exceptional dedi-cation," Captain Pierce said, his grin reaching his eyes, which crinkled at the edges in genuine delight. "I appreciate you bringing this to my attention."

Once they had bid the captain farewell and were en route to their respective cabins, Gemma couldn't help but look speculatively toward Viv. "You certainly put on quite the show back there."

With a mischievous glint in her eye, Viv winked at her companion. "Darling, in times like these, sometimes you've got to bend the story a bit to catch a break—or, in this case, to catch a killer."

Gemma's cane tapped a steady rhythm as they navigated the crowds toward the Grand Dining Hall.

"Viv," Gemma began, her voice low and steady as they approached the dining hall, "I truly appreciate what you did for Meg, but why spin such a tale? You barely know her."

Viv laughed, a bright peal that seemed to make the surrounding passengers glance their way with curiosity. Her eyes met Gemma's as they walked side by side. "Meg isn't spinning yarns. I had myself a heart-to-heart with Rob, that blackjack dealer she's sweet on. Poor fella was jittery, but I laid it out straight—the mess Meg could land in without his honesty. He caved, corroborated her story down to the letter, and whipped out his phone to show me their selfie from the previous evening."

Gemma felt an unexpected pang of relief; it was one less worry if Meg, indeed, was innocent.

"And as for why," Viv continued with a glimmer of mischief in her eyes, "I was up late myself, strolling with my favorite bartender, Alex." She gave a playful wink. "He kept his favorite mature Vegas performer company—a perfect gentleman. Not quite a scene from Titanic, but good enough to keep me up past my recommended bedtime.

"I'll have to introduce you two later. Besides, what did I tell you? Any friend of yours is a friend of mine," Viv said warmly, affectionately squeezing Gemma's hand.

The gesture caught Gemma off guard; she wasn't used to

such displays. Yet she couldn't deny the warmth that spread through her at the sentiment.

Entering the dining hall, Brent Li escorted the two women to a corner table. Dinner unfolded around them with its usual pomp and circumstance. Chef Jane Duffy came out to personally greet guests with her warm smile as the wait-staff moved like clockwork around the long tables adorned with white linens.

Elegantly dressed diners engaged in hushed conversations against a backdrop of ocean views through the sweeping glass windows.

A waiter, impeccable in uniform and graceful in movement, approached to gather their culinary preferences and replenish their glasses with chilled water. As the server departed, Gemma embraced the brief interlude of tranquility, mentally preparing to strategize their subsequent actions.

"Well," she said decisively, "with Meg's name soon to be cleared thanks to your clever thinking, we must focus on finding who else had reason to end Valentina's career...and life."

Viv nodded resolutely. "Alrighty then, Sherlock," Viv quipped, her green eyes shimmering with mischief. "What's next?"

CHAPTER 11

"I know where we should start," Viv leaned forward, a radiant glow suffusing her cheeks as she rubbed her hands together. "Lady Luck is smiling on us tonight. What do you say we hit the casino?"

Gemma cocked her head, eyeing Viv with a mixture of admiration and bewilderment. The casino had never been on her radar on land or sea; the mere thought of it was as foreign as skydiving or bull riding. But Viv's enthusiasm was infectious, and Gemma couldn't help but be swayed by the vibrant woman's adventurous spirit. "Well, I suppose it wouldn't hurt to observe…"

"Observe? Sugar, we're going to dive in!" Viv looped her arm through Gemma's, guiding them back to their rooms. "Meet me at the casino in forty minutes, dressed to impress —or at least as jazzy as you can muster."

Back in her cabin, Gemma faced her modest wardrobe with a frown. She didn't dress to impress; she dressed to be neat, presentable, and comfortable. She had packed for up to a year of cruising with a sensible assortment of easily mixed and matched outfits in neutral colors. What does one wear to a casino? She settled on a navy skirt paired with a cream blouse and draped a soft gray cardigan over her shoulders for warmth. The ensemble was classic, if not slightly drab—especially considering what Viv might appear in.

True to form, Viv awaited Gemma at the casino entrance, clad in a daring black dress. Gemma marveled at the gravity-defying garment, hugging Viv's curves, pondering the required engineering.

"Ah, there you are!" Viv exclaimed. "You look lovely—like an English rose among these glitzy tulips."

Gemma's lips curved into a wry smile, skepticism flickering in her gray eyes. Besides Viv's glamour, she felt like a schoolmarm standing with a screen siren from Hollywood's golden era. What on earth did Viv find in her that sparked such an eager partnership in sleuthing—and now, in the art of gambling?

Before she could ponder that question, Viv whisked them through the buzzing casino floor, which was filled with bright lights and clattering chips. Gemma's senses tingled at the cacophony of slot machines and the soft rustle of cards against green baize.

"Look who's here," Viv chirped as they approached a blackjack table. A muscular man with curly honey-blonde hair, a thick gold necklace, and a hint of a tattoo peeking out under his white polo shirt stood dealing cards with an easy smile. Gemma observed the worry that creased his brow, framing his blue eyes with lines of concern.

"Good evening, ladies," he greeted them. "I hope you're both doing well tonight."

"I'm fantastic, Rob," Viv chirped. "I'm doing even better now that I had a chance to tell Captain Pierce about the marvelous hospitality Meg gave me late last night."

Rob's eyebrows shot up, and he stopped dealing cards to

look at the older woman with a mixture of confusion and wonder.

"Yes, indeed, Meg is a credit to the cruise industry. She stayed up long past her bedtime to walk the decks with this insomniac until three in the morning and made sure I was snug as a bug in my cabin. Such a lovely conversationalist she is."

"Viv, you didn't," Rob breathed as he swallowed hard and resumed dealing with the small group.

"The Captain should know how fine his staff is," Viv said, tapping the table for the next card. "I might also put in a good word for you, sugar cakes. It depends on how the cards go tonight, I guess."

Rob's face brightened considerably; gratitude replaced concern as he reached under the table and presented them with a handful of free tokens.

"You've no idea what this means to us," he said earnestly. "I owe you one."

"Just make sure you treat our girl right," Viv wagged a finger at him playfully. "And get cracking on changing those outdated staff rules!"

Rob's chuckle rippled through the air, a sound of easy assurance. "You have my word," he declared with a wink, fingers dancing over the cards as he shuffled the deck with the flourish of a magician setting the stage for their next round of play.

"I don't believe you've had the pleasure of making Mrs. Gemma Becker's acquaintance, have you?" Viv swept her hand toward her friend, her bracelets jangling like a chime.

"Meg told me about you," Rob said, acknowledging Gemma respectfully. "How you helped her after Valentina's outburst. It meant more to her than you know, and well, it meant a lot to me, since Meg and I—" He cut off, a rosy hue dusting his cheeks as he averted his eyes.

Gemma waved a dismissive hand, the corners of her mouth twitching upward.

"Think nothing of it. Guests disrespecting good staff is one thing I cannot abide. Viv may know her way around these cards, but I fear I am rather a novice. Could you spare a moment to teach an old lady a new trick?"

"Certainly, ma'am," Rob replied with a warm grin. "It's quite straightforward once you get the hang of it."

Rob's explanation flowed with the ease of someone well-versed in the game, turning complex rules into simple steps. Before long, Gemma's focus sharpened, and she began assessing her cards with a strategic eye. She calculated her moves precisely, and to her delight, her stack of chips swiftly grew to twice its original size.

Other casino visitors slipped away to try their luck at other tables, such as roulette, poker, or slot machines.

"Luck be a lady tonight, Gemma," Viv sang, her voice carrying the husky timbre of a seasoned showgirl. "Keep up the sharp eye, and you'll have this case wrapped up with a bow."

Rob arched a brow and leaned closer, his voice a low murmur. "So, are you two masterminds stitching together the mystery of Valentina's untimely demise?"

Viv flashed a grin, mischief sparkling in her eyes. "Oh, we're deep in it," she confirmed. "Haven't had a thrill like this on the high seas since I was called to improvise a show during a blackout!"

Rob leaned in closer, dropping his voice to a conspiratorial murmur. "You didn't hear it from me, but I saw something that night, but I couldn't exactly tell just anyone," He glanced around before continuing. "I know you're the soul of discretion, Viv, and any friend of yours is a friend of mine."

Viv and Gemma edged nearer, their breaths suspended in a mix of anticipation.

"Henri, that French wine guy, was out late that night, too. Meg and I saw him staggering towards Valentina's quarters well after midnight. He had something in his hands, too—bulky looking. I couldn't make it out, but I know it was him."

Viv hoisted a skeptical brow. By her side, Gemma absorbed the revelation without a word, her mind whirring with the implications.

As other guests gathered around the table, Rob bid them farewell with a conspiratorial nod.

"Well, well, well," Viv purred, a glint of mischief sparkling in her green eyes. "If that isn't a juicy development," she said.

"Indeed," Gemma concurred, her voice steady yet tinged with a hint of excitement. "A drink seems in order, wouldn't you say?"

* * *

GEMMA EYED the glitzy casino bar, a mosaic of lights reflecting off polished glassware and bottles of every conceivable liquor. The sounds of the casino melded into a symphony of clinking chips, whirring slots, and the occasional cheer from a winning streak. In her daring black number, Viv sashayed up to the bar with the confidence of a woman who knew every stage and audience.

"One Moscow Mule, darling," Viv said to the bartender, her voice ringing with the same vibrato she might have used on stage.

Gemma approached more tentatively. "Just a ginger ale for me, please."

Viv turned to her with a smirk that crinkled the corners of her eyes. "Ginger ale? At this hour? Gemma, live a little."

"Boring, my dear Viv, has been a rather reliable companion for sixty-four years," Gemma quipped with a defiant lift of her chin, accepting the sparkling ginger ale from the bartender. "Besides, with all the intrigue aboard this vessel, it's best I keep my wits sharp."

They chose a table with a vantage point that allowed them to survey the sea of patrons mingling among blackjack tables and roulette wheels. Settling into their seats, Gemma took a sip from her cool drink—the sharpness of ginger tickling her throat—while Viv sipped delicately at the icy spiced drink in her frosty copper mug.

"We've got quite the tangle to unravel," Gemma murmured, watching guests flit from table to table.

Viv leaned in closer. "Let's lay it all out then."

"Henri was loitering near Valentina's cabin after hours, with something bulky in his arms, no less."

"And he was her 'biggest fan,'" Viv added air quotes. "He told us of the special brew he made for her. Could he have poisoned a bottle out of obsession or spiteful anger?"

"Perhaps," Gemma mused. "Until an autopsy can be performed, we're only guessing. It's entirely in the realm of possibility. Then there's Dirk." Gemma tapped her finger on the table. "Their public spats were no secret, so you say."

"Oh, they are legendary. Plus, he's got that temper, and Valentina had no problem pushing all his buttons." Viv swirled her drink. "A deadly combination, if you ask me."

"And Piper?"

"You saw her last night at the show. I doubt there's any love for her now-former boss. She could've snapped under Valentina's tyranny."

Gemma nodded slowly. "We need more than speculation, though. We need facts—alibis, motives…"

Viv tapped her lip thoughtfully. "We need more intel."

"Exactly," Gemma concurred, her empty glass making a soft clink as she placed it firmly on the table. "Only who will spill the proverbial beans to mere passengers like us?"

CHAPTER 12

The first rays of dawn slanted through the porthole, casting a warm glow over the room. Gemma stirred, the early morning light caressing the oval photo on her bedside table and lingering on the face of the young man behind the glass. Her Tom, forever young, forever missed. Nestled at the foot of her bed, Buddy sensed her awakening and wiggled to her side with a soft whine.

Her body ached from yesterday's exertion in the aqua fit class, each muscle groaning in protest as she sat up. She rose carefully, joints stiff and uncooperative. She eased into gentle stretches, hoping to coax flexibility back into her limbs. As she moved, she mulled over the events that had transpired: Viv's audacious yet compassionate lie that provided Meg and Rob with alibis, Rob's revelation regarding Henri's furtive late-night stumblings in the vicinity of Valentina's room, and their need for more information. But from whom?

As she extended her arm, the room spun unexpectedly. Gemma's hand shot out, finding purchase on the cool surface of the wall, anchoring her until the short-lived dizzy spell

. a long, weary exhale, she abandoned plans for
.neal in the bustling dining hall. Instead, she
solace in preparing her own Earl Grey, her cabin
ry from the ship's constant activity. She cast a
glance at the day's schedule, a flicker of amusement
g her features.

British Tea will be served at four o'clock in the Rose
ng Hall," she mused aloud, her voice tinged with
iosity and skepticism. "I suppose I must attend, if only to
sess whether this American vessel can meet the mark."

There was a knock at the door as she waited for the kettle
to signal its readiness. It was Meg, eyes brimming with
gratitude.

"Mrs. Becker," Meg began in a whisper, wringing her
hands together. "I can't stay long. I heard what you did. I
don't know how to thank you for everything you've done for
Rob and me."

Gemma waved off her thanks with a gentle smile. "It was
Viv who saved the day," she said softly. "I'll pass along your
gratitude when I see her."

Meg nodded. "I was asked to drop this off for you," she
said, placing a folded note in Gemma's hand. With a swift,
apologetic smile, she turned on her heel and hurried down
the corridor, her figure soon swallowed by the bustle of the
ship's activity.

Gemma secured the door behind her and retreated into
the solace of her cabin. She unfolded the note in the hush,
revealing a message in hurried penmanship.

Good morning, beautiful!

*I would have sent you a text, but you had to be the one person
on this entire ship that doesn't have a phone. Snail mail, it will
have to be then, my old-fashioned friend. Meet me for brunch at 11
on the rooftop cafe. I found someone with some dirt to dish. You
won't want to miss this!*

xo
Viv

"Everyone who needs me has always been able to reach me all these years," Gemma remarked wryly. "I don't see why I need a phone constantly ringing in my pocket for others' convenience." Buddy wagged his tail in response.

The kettle click caught her attention, and she poured steaming water over her teabag. The aroma of citrus and bergamot enveloped her, prompting a contented sigh. The morning stretched ahead, a luxurious expanse of solitude before the promised revelations of brunch. She settled into the plush contours of her armchair, the heat from her mug seeping into her palms.

She glanced at Buddy, who sat attentively at her feet. "Now, whom do you think Viv found to dish out the dirt?"

AT FIVE TO ELEVEN, Gemma eased into a white wicker chair at the rooftop cafe, her trusty Buddy settling down happily by her side with his tongue lolling out in a soft doggy smile. Viv swept onto the rooftop mere seconds later, her presence a vivid splash against the cafe's muted tones. Her lemon-yellow sundress clung to her with summer ease, a wide-brimmed white hat perched atop her head, framing her face in a chic halo. Glamorous black sunglasses shielded her eyes, casting elegant shadows along her high cheekbones. At her heels, Fernando trotted with a dignified air, his yellow kerchief knotted smartly around his neck in a flamboyant echo of Viv's effervescent style.

"Goodness, Vivian, you've turned the dog into a fashion accessory," Gemma quipped, smoothing her sensible tan skirt as the waiter came and took their orders.

Viv laughed heartily, patting the seat next to her. "Well, if

79

I'm going to do anything, I might as well do it in style. My dear Gemma, you really must join this century. I can't believe I had to write you a letter. I can't even remember the last time I did that."

Gemma bristled slightly at the suggestion. "My dear Vivian, life without those incessant beeps and buzzes has kept me quite content. I have no urge to take photos of myself, no one I care to show my photos to, nor do I need to know what everyone is doing at every moment of the day. I see no reason to change now."

Viv shook her head, amused. "Your stubbornness is part of your charm, I suppose." She leaned forward conspiratorially. "So, curious about our brunch companion?"

"Is the Pope Catholic?"

Before Gemma could say more, Viv waved over a willowy, dark-haired lady approaching their table. The woman hesitated momentarily before joining them, her dark eyes darting between Buddy and Fernando as she sat.

"Gemma Becker, meet Nina Pavlova," Viv announced with a flourish. "This morning, I was bereft of your delightful commentary on the superiority of British blends compared to herbal tea, so I invited myself to the chorus girls' breakfast table. We had the most interesting conversation about the one and only Valentina."

Nina smiled shyly and swept a loose strand of her dark hair behind her ear. Gemma gave her a warm smile and nodded toward Viv, who responded by toasting the air with orange juice.

"Nina, your tenure with the chorus—how long have you been with the opera?" Gemma inquired.

"About seven years," Nina answered. "I went to Juilliard and always had my heart set on working with the greats. Working for the New York Opera House has been a dream, and now, traveling on a fancy cruise ship like this one is double awesome. The only hard part has been…"

"Valentina?" Viv finished.

"Valentina was…complicated," Nina began delicately.

"Like all headliners, she's, well, was, a bit of a prima donna. She's been with the company for three years and sells out all the shows. No one but those of us who worked with her knows what a train wreck she was."

Viv leaned in. "Tell us everything."

Gemma's gray eyes sharpened, her attention unwavering as Nina sketched a portrait of Valentina DeLuca in words—a star whose brilliance on stage was undeniable, yet behind the curtains she loomed, an imposing figure whose grace faded when dealing with subordinates.

Nina's eyes darted around the room before she continued, the strain evident in her hushed tones. "The way she spoke to Piper was demeaning, utterly disrespectful. And Dirk, well, he didn't escape her wrath either."

Gemma tilted her head, her curiosity piqued. "Were they at odds then, Dirk and Valentina?"

The corners of Nina's lips twitched with the weight of unspoken stories. She leaned in further, ensuring their huddle was private. "Let's just say they shook the walls with their 'discussions,'" she revealed. "As for the nature of their relationship, it's anyone's guess. But you know what they say —where there's smoke, there's fire."

Viv leaned in closer. "And who steps into Valentina's shoes tonight? The show must go on."

Casting a wary eye over her shoulder, Nina lowered her voice before replying. "It's common knowledge—we've all memorized her roles. Anyone could take center stage tonight. Dirk will tell us any minute now."

Before Gemma could ask any more questions, their

conversation halted as a young woman burst onto the terrace.

"Nina," she exclaimed, breathless and flushed with urgency.

"You won't believe what just happened."

CHAPTER 13

The chorus member, breathless from excitement and the brisk walk up to the rooftop cafe, slid into the chair beside Nina with eyes wide. "You won't believe it," she whispered, leaning forward. "Lucia Rossi is stepping in for Valentina tonight and every night until we hit New York!"

Nina's reaction was a mixture of surprise and congratulations. "Lucia? Well, that's fantastic! She's got a voice that could make angels weep."

The willowy brunette leaned back, glancing over her shoulder before confiding in them. "But between us, it's odd. Lucia landed the lead role very conveniently."

Viv's eyebrows arched in interest. "You think she played her cards right? With Dirk?"

Nina shrugged, yet her eyes held a gleam of implied scandal. Her voice dropped to a conspiratorial murmur. "Dirk does have a certain fondness for the many talents of his singers." Her voice tapered into silence, the insinuation hanging in the air, an unfinished thought ripe with suggestion.

Gemma and Viv exchanged looks as another layer was added to this tapestry of intrigue. Nina excused herself and left with the other chorus member, their heads bent low together.

Gemma sipped her tea thoughtfully as Viv cooed at Fernando under the table. Across the rooftop café, passengers chatted, basking in the mid-morning sun that cast a glittering sheen on the ocean beyond, seemingly oblivious to the fact that a murderer was aboard.

"That was quite the dish of dirt," Gemma remarked, retrieving her list from the depths of her purse. She ran her eyes over the notations they'd compiled, each a breadcrumb on the trail of deceit woven through the ship's corridors.

"It's my pleasure, hon," Viv replied with a twinkle in her eye, leaning in closer. "Better add Lucia to the list, Mrs. Becker. She's as tangled in this web as a fish in a net."

"My thoughts exactly, Ms. Carlisle," Gemma concurred, her pen poised above the paper before the name 'Lucia Rossi' joined the growing list of suspects.

Gemma's fingers danced delicately across the page, lingering on each suspect's name as if to glean more from their inked impressions. There was Dirk, whose volatile outbursts and wandering gaze had long marked him as suspect material; Piper, whose disdain was as frequent as her breaths, her eyes perpetually skyward in silent judgment; and Henri, whose nocturnal bumbling had not gone unnoticed. And now, Lucia's name settled onto the page, adding another layer to the intricate puzzle.

"Penny for your thoughts?"

Gemma slipped the list in her purse and looked up. "I'm weighing our facts against our fiction," she replied. "The devil's in the details, and we're dancing with quite a few here."

Viv leaned in closer, her gaze sharp despite her striking exterior.

"So what's our next play?"

Gemma tapped her lips with her pen. "We need to learn more about Lucia Rossi's relationship with Dirk. More than ambition may have driven her to replace Valentina violently."

Viv nodded, her eyes gleaming with intrigue. "What about the chorus girls?" she said. "Jealousy can fester like a bad wound."

"That it can," Gemma agreed, jotting another note on the list.

Viv looked over Gemma's shoulder. "Uh oh. Here comes trouble."

Security Chief Grimshaw strode toward Gemma and Viv with the kind of purpose that caused the surrounding passengers to part like the Red Sea. He fixed his gaze on them, his lips a tight line of disapproval.

"Mrs. Becker, Ms. Carlisle," he barked, the sharpness in his tone unmistakable. "I can't help but notice you're once again sticking your noses where they do not belong."

Viv's smile sparkled with feigned sweetness as she batted her eyelashes. "Chief Grimshaw, surely we're entitled to a bit of harmless chatter, aren't we? Or has the ship's policy changed regarding pleasantries among passengers?"

Grimshaw leaned in, hands clasped behind his back. "You know very well what I'm talking about. Meddling with my investigation is no game for retirees to pass the time."

Gemma observed him coolly from behind her spectacles. "Surely your inquiry is robust enough to withstand a bit of civilian curiosity," she said.

His eyes narrowed. "Don't play coy with me. I saw you chatting up that chorus girl, Nina. You're collecting information like you're set to solve this case before me."

Viv's laughter danced through the air, light and teasing.

"Oh, relax. We're just gossiping over eggs and mimosas. Harmless fun."

Grimshaw's face reddened as if they had lit a fire beneath his collar. "Harmless? I heard about your alibi for Meg," he accused Viv directly. "And I don't buy it for one second."

Gemma interjected before Viv could retort, her voice firm but calm. "Do you have any evidence for that?"

He snorted and pointed the finger at them both, "Mark my words; if you two don't keep out of ship security business, I'll stop this ship in Iceland and leave you there to think about meddling in matters beyond your pay grade."

The threat hung heavy in the air for a moment before Grimshaw continued with a smug tone, "I may not have evidence to expose Ms. Carlisle's story," he leaned closer as if divulging state secrets, "I do, however, have access to video footage that you wannabe detectives don't." He paused for effect, his chest puffing slightly with pride.

"Then, I'm sure you know all about Henri being near Valentina's cabin that night," Viv jutted her chin, challenging him to continue.

His control slipped as he blurted out, "Henri wasn't just 'in the vicinity.' The fool was caught on camera stumbling down the hall and knocking on Valentina's door. Left her a little gift, he did!"

Grimshaw's face flushed red while Gemma exchanged a knowing glance with Viv, an unspoken conversation passing between them. He spun on his heel and stormed off in a huff, leaving an air of indignation swirling in his wake.

Gemma watched him go and then turned to Viv with an amused twinkle in her eye.

"Well," Viv sighed dramatically but with an unmistakable glint of excitement, "he sure knows how to make an exit."

"And you know how to goad a man into revealing his secrets," Gemma said appreciatively.

Viv curled her lips into a sly grin. "Let's just say I've coaxed a secret or two out of a gentleman or two in my time."

"I'd be willing to wager that gift was a bottle of wine from Valentina's biggest fan," Gemma remarked. "It was the same special blend he said he had been working on for months, just for his muse."

Viv nodded knowingly.

"He may have access to cameras," Gemma pondered aloud while discreetly noting the latest revelation about Henri on her list, "but we have something Grimshaw lacks—discretion and charm."

"Good breath and fabulous style," Viv added with a grin before becoming more serious. "But did you see his face? I wonder how much pressure he's under to solve this quickly."

Gemma's nod came slow, pensive. "A mere four days until we dock in New York. Not much of a window for him—or us—to unravel this mystery."

Viv casually leaned back in her chair, folding her arms behind her head. "Well, I'm not going to let Mr. Corn Cob get me down; this is the most fun I've had on any cruise."

Gemma smiled in agreement as she placed her pen beside her teacup. For her, it wasn't just about fun, but also truth and justice.

"What Father Brown Would Do," she mused aloud as if reading Viv's thoughts.

"That detective priest?" Viv asked.

"The one and only," Gemma looked out over the deck where passengers lounged in carefree bliss, unaware of the drama unfolding around them.

"He would bring truth, justice, and order wherever he found himself." Her eyes met Viv's again. "However he could, wherever he could."

"And that's exactly what we're going to do," Viv said resolutely.

She slipped the carefully compiled list into the inner pocket of her purse, its corners crisp and purposeful.

Rising to their feet, they drew the attention of Buddy, who looked up with a keen sense, his tail a rhythmic pendulum expressing his shared anticipation.

Viv leaned closer, a conspiratorial gleam in her eye. "But first," she murmured, the hush of her voice tinged with the thrill of the chase, "there's a little matter we need to attend to."

CHAPTER 14

*T*he glint in Viv's eyes was unmistakable; she had another scheme brewing.

With a mischievous twinkle, Viv stretched her arms above her head. "This showgirl's limbs are begging for a stretch, and I know just the spot." Her grin widened in anticipation.

Gemma's expression fell, her mind conjuring a whirlwind of bizarre possibilities Viv might have up her sleeve. Would it be aquatic jogging with overly enthusiastic retirees, belly dancing to the relentless rhythms of some exotic beat, or even contorting into unnatural poses among the ship's more limber guests?

"You'll thank me, hon," Viv assured her, eyes glinting with the promise of their latest escapade. "There's this new exercise instructor on board, Bonnie something or other, with a stellar reputation for getting results, German style. And trust me, a good stretch does wonders for us, especially after yesterday's splashing around and shuffleboard antics. We deserve a treat, and Bonnie's class is the talk of the ship!"

Gemma arched an eyebrow, but a small part of her could

not deny the stiffness in her limbs. Despite the apprehension knotting in her stomach, she couldn't help but admire Viv's relentless energy. "I suppose I could use some loosening up," she conceded.

"Perfect!" Viv clapped her hands together. "Change into something you can move in and meet me in the fitness room in thirty minutes. This will be so much fun!"

Gemma couldn't suppress a groan as she returned to her cabin with Buddy in tow. "That Vivian and I have distinctly different definitions of fun," she muttered. "I might thank or kill that infernal woman later."

Once in her room, Gemma reluctantly slipped into comfortable workout attire—nothing too revealing or garish —and ensured Buddy had plenty of water and a chew toy to keep him company. "Wish me luck, Buddy," she murmured, giving his head an affectionate pat. "I'm going to need it." The door closed behind her with a soft click, leaving Buddy to his devices.

Outside the fitness center, Viv was sporting neon leggings and a tank top that read 'Retired but not Expired.' Gemma, in black loose-fitting pants and a white T-shirt, felt positively drab next to her.

Gemma and Viv crossed the threshold into the fitness center, immediately enveloped by an energetic cacophony of participants warming up. The space was alive, filled with the hum of conversation and rhythmic thuds of sneakers compressing the springy floor. A motley crew assembled: female retirees with jaws set in steely resolve, middle-aged women with the vibrant glow of endorphins already upon their faces, and a smattering of men, their postures a cocktail of hesitancy and bravado claimed their territory of the mats. United in purpose, each was poised to conquer the morning workout.

"Ready to get whipped into shape, Gem?" Viv teased with a nudge, her eyes sparkling with mischief.

Gemma shot her a wry glance. "If I collapse, promise you'll drag me to the nearest lifeboat and set me adrift. It'd be a mercy."

Viv laughed heartily. "Darling, we'll be two peas in a pod, wobbling out of here together. But think of the buffet rewards!"

With that, they joined the others, their anticipation mingling with trepidation as Bonnie, whistle in hand, stepped forward to begin. The fitness instructor, unmistakable with her platinum blonde pixie cut accented by whimsical pink tips, strode confidently to the front of the class. Her whistle glinted around her neck as she introduced herself with a voice that cut through the noise, "*Guten Tag!* I'm Bonnie Hertz, and I'll be your tormentor—I mean, instructor—for today's session." The room erupted in laughter and groans, but all eyes were fixed on her as she exuded an aura of intimidation and motivation.

"We'll start with some limbering exercises, and once we're warmed up, prepare to discover stretching in a whole new way."

Viv's usually relaxed demeanor wavered at the veiled assurance lacing Bonnie's words. The moment for reflection was fleeting; the class surged into motion with limbering drills. As they lunged and swung, squatted, and stretched, Gemma discovered muscles she never knew she had.

"Heavens above," Gemma hissed at Viv as sweat broke out over their foreheads. "Is she going to stretch us or kill us?"

Gemma felt herself being pulled into positions that seemed entirely unnatural for human anatomy. She gritted her teeth and tried to focus on breathing as Bonnie made another lap around the room.

"You there!" Bonnie barked suddenly in Gemma's direction. "More effort! You must feel the stretch. Be willing to do the reps, run the late-night laps, and feel the burn!"

Gemma could feel the stretch—every muscle screamed in protest as she pushed further into the pose.

Viv shot Gemma an apologetic smile from where she contorted herself with surprising grace.

"Remind me to never listen to you again," Gemma whispered through clenched teeth as she transitioned to another painful stretch.

Viv's giggle escaped just as the platinum Amazonian towered over them. "This is not comedy club!" she snapped. "To get results with Bonnie Hertz, you must focus."

"I never expected stretching to *hurt* so much," Gemma quipped dryly, unable to resist playing on Bonnie's surname.

Viv's composure crumbled into a cascade of snickers, each giggle punctuated by an unbridled snort echoing through the room.

Bonnie's face turned an impressive shade of crimson as she stood with hands on hips, glaring at them both. "If you cannot take my instruction seriously, you can leave!"

Catching sight of Viv, now practically folded in half with laughter, Gemma was struck by the absurdity of the moment. A chuckle slipped out despite her efforts to stifle it, and she swiftly covered her mouth with her hand.

Tears streaming down her face, Viv motioned her with her hand for them to leave. The two flushed women gathered their things under the watchful eyes of the class and made their way out, still chuckling between themselves.

Outside in the hallway, free from Bonnie's stern gaze, they burst into laughter again—this time uncontained and hearty.

"Fancy that," Gemma managed between breaths. "I haven't laughed like this in years."

Viv wiped tears from her eyes. "See? I told you stretching

would make you feel better. Laughter is the best medicine, they say."

Gemma shook her head, the corners of her mouth twitching into a bemused smile. "An abdominal workout was not the morning stretch I had in mind," she remarked, the laughter still dancing in her eyes. "At least it got us out of that infernal class early."

As their laughter died down and they caught their breaths, Viv patted Gemma on the back with affectionate camaraderie.

"Come on," she said with a wink, "let's go find something less painful to do."

Gemma's muscles protested with every step because of Bonnie's relentless regime. They had just reached the door, the sweet taste of escape within reach, when a young man in crisp whites approached with a tray.

"Mango smoothies, ladies?" he offered, a bright smile adorning his youthful face.

Gemma eyed the thick golden liquid, contemplating the pros and cons. Her body ached for something soothing. "Your timing is impeccable, sir," she murmured and accepted one. The smoothie was a refreshing balm to her palate, the tropical flavors mingling with the salt in the air.

"Don't mind if I do," Viv snatched one as well, raising her glass in a silent toast to the ocean sprawling beyond the panoramic windows. "Here's to surviving Bonnie 'Make It Hurt' and her chamber of stretching horrors," she quipped.

A chuckle escaped Gemma before she could stifle it. Viv's words tickled her humor just right. They stood side by side, sipping their smoothies and gazing at the infinite blue. The laughter faded into a comfortable silence as Gemma reflected on the camaraderie forming between them.

She hadn't laughed like this in years—genuine, unguarded mirth. Not since her Tom had been alive to appreciate her dry remarks over morning tea. A pang of sorrow laced with sweetness ached in her chest at the memory. For so long, laughter had been a stranger to her lips. Now, through Viv's infectious spirit, it felt like reacquainting with an old friend.

"Your puns are sharper than Bonnie's whistle," Viv said, breaking into Gemma's reverie with an appreciative grin.

"Oh, it was nothing," Gemma replied, but inwardly, she basked in the warmth of shared amusement. It was a novel sensation—this ease of interaction without expectations or obligations.

Viv's playful smirk shifted into another jab at their instructor. "Imagine if Bonnie applied her zeal for reps to solving this mystery—she'd have Piper doing push-ups until she confessed!"

The image sparked an idea within Gemma. "Bonnie," she murmured under her breath.

"What about her?" Viv tilted her head curiously.

"She said something about last night that—"

Gemma glanced at the dispersing crowd from their class, noting Bonnie collecting mats with military precision. "I need to speak with Bonnie again—and soon."

Viv nodded. "Leave it to me," she said with a conspiratorial wink, pulling Gemma into the fitness room.

Viv dramatically approached Bonnie, clasping her hands together as if pleading for absolution. "You'll have to excuse Gemma," Viv said, her voice carrying a theatrical somberness. "She hasn't been herself since everything that's happened."

Bonnie looked up from her task and regarded Gemma through narrowed eyes that slowly softened. She nodded once, firmly yet not unkindly. "Stress can wreak havoc on one's wellbeing," she acknowledged. "Perhaps you should try low-impact walking—it's far less strenuous than my classes… or my midnight jogs."

"Did you happen to go for one such jog on the night Valentina died?" Gemma inquired casually, masking the intensity of her curiosity.

Bonnie paused before answering as if discussing the weather.

"Of course," she affirmed, her accent subtly betraying her German heritage. "I always go for a solid one-hour run, sometimes more, at midnight. I have conditioned my body only to need five hours of sleep."

Viv rolled her eyes subtly at Bonnie's self-congratulatory tone but said nothing.

Gemma leaned in, "Did you happen to see anything unusual during your run?"

Bonnie's steel-blue gaze hesitated momentarily—a flicker of something unreadable before it vanished behind her disciplined facade.

"*Ja*," Bonnie started slowly as if recalling each detail with precision. "I saw a young blonde woman doing something strange."

Gemma and Viv leaned in simultaneously while Bonnie took a deliberate sip from her water bottle.

"Something strange indeed." The fitness instructor set down her bottle and wiped an invisible speck of dust from her perfectly ironed hot pink tank top before locking eyes with both women. "Something I've never seen before."

CHAPTER 15

*B*onnie Hertz towered over them, a pillar of athletic discipline, as she brushed back a lock of her platinum hair, tinged with pink. "It was after my late-night laps. I saw that little blondie who was always with Madame Valentina sneaking to the back of the ship with a large duffel bag," she said, blowing her whistle lightly as if to punctuate. "I have no idea what her business was at that late hour, but I was on track to shatter my record. No time to stop and chat."

Gemma's eyes widened behind her wire-rimmed glasses. She had known there was more to the assistant than met the eye. "Thank you, Bonnie," Gemma nodded, "for the stretch and information. It was most educational."

Viv pressed a hand to her lips, stifling a chuckle behind a well-timed cough.

Once outside the fitness area, Gemma and Viv walked side by side in silence for a moment.

"A large duffel bag? What on earth could Piper be lugging around at such an ungodly hour?" Gemma pondered aloud.

Viv's green eyes sparkled with mischief. "Maybe she's got

Valentina's secret stash of jewels? Or maybe she was throwing evidence overboard?"

Gemma shook her head; the notion seemed far-fetched yet strangely plausible. "Not a dead body, obviously," she quipped dryly, earning Viv a hearty laugh.

The ship's corridors welcomed them back like old friends as they approached the elevator bay. Gemma thought about the duffel bag and what it could contain. Stolen items? Incriminating documents? Risque pool toys? The possibilities swirled in her mind like tea leaves in a cup.

"Ah yes, tea," Gemma said as they stepped into an elevator, "I meant to tell you, Viv. This good ship has an excellent item on the schedule today that may prove worthwhile. A proper British Tea shall be hosted in one of the smaller dining halls in half an hour. Fancy a nibble?"

Viv perked up at that. "Is the Captain a dreamboat? Count me in! I could use a bit of pampering after that stretch session with Sergeant Hertz."

Gemma smiled at Viv's comment and nodded in agreement as she took her leave.

Back in her room, Gemma surveyed her wardrobe with a practiced eye, settling on a classic beige blouse paired with a matching skirt that suggested elegance without pretense. She brushed her steel gray hair, coaxing it into gentle curls that framed her face with a touch of softness. A small, tasteful hat, reminiscent of the late Queen's style, perched neatly atop her head. Lastly, she secured a vintage cameo brooch at her collar. A final approving glance in the mirror confirmed she was ready for the afternoon's genteel affair.

She glanced at Buddy, his coat a tad unkempt from the day's earlier exploits. With a tender motion, she retrieved his grooming brush from the nightstand and tapped the edge of the bed, a silent summons. He responded with a wagging tail, bounding onto the soft comforter. Ensuring she and her faithful companion exuded sophistication, she meticulously groomed his fur. After all, afternoon tea demanded a certain decorum, and Buddy was to be no exception.

Looking at Buddy carefully, she wondered momentarily if a kerchief might suit him. Perhaps a nice red to match his lovely brown? "Oh, pish posh," she scolded herself. "If I don't watch myself, I'll dress him in tweed coats and blazers. That Viv is having an ill effect on me."

Dismissing the idea, Gemma completed her freshening up and met Viv outside her cabin moments later. Viv had transformed into something much more colorful than Gemma would ever wear—a vibrant floral dress smattered with blooms. They went to the smaller dining hall where the High Tea was set up. The room buzzed softly with conversation and clinking china. Waiters glided between tables, offering steaming pots of tea and plates laden with scones, sandwiches, and delicate pastries.

The aroma of Orange Pekoe tea enveloped Gemma, a comforting embrace as she nestled into her seat, Buddy curling contentedly at her feet. Their table, graced with crisp white linen, showcased gleaming silver service that caught the glow of the subdued lighting. Fresh flowers floated in shallow water-filled vessels, adding a touch of elegance. For a moment, Gemma felt perfectly at home.

Viv whistled as she surveyed the spread before them. "I gotta say, Gemma dear, this is quite impressive," she remarked as she picked up a dainty cucumber sandwich.

Gemma beamed with pride at Viv's approval; this was her element—etiquette and elegance intertwined like vines in an English garden.

A uniformed waiter delivered a steaming pot of tea, and Gemma inhaled its rich aroma, allowing it to linger before cautiously tasting. "That will do," she conceded, adding a splash of milk and swirling her spoon with deliberate care.

As they sipped their tea, Gemma was surprised to feel contentment wash over her like warm sunlight through a windowpane. The investigation had brought unexpected excitement into her retirement. She honestly had not laughed like that since…Tom. Had it been so long? The years had slipped into decades, and now she saw the face of an old woman looking back at her in the mirror each day. Where had the time gone?

"You look like you're going down memory lane there, hon," Viv remarked as she split a scone in half.

Gemma cleared her throat and composed her face. "It must be the cucumber sandwiches bringing me home," she replied. "Never mind my wandering thoughts; let us apply ourselves to the only good thing to come from Miss Hurts-Alot's class."

Viv glanced at her knowingly. "Sure, hon. Cucumbers do that." She spooned strawberry jam onto her scone halves. "We can talk about other things."

"Yes, let's." Gemma passed her the clotted cream. "So Piper was sneaking around on the top deck after midnight with a large duffel bag containing unknown artifacts."

"It doesn't necessarily pin her as the murderer," Viv countered with a thoughtful frown. "She could be smuggling contraband, ditching evidence, or rendezvousing with a secret someone. This vessel was practically buzzing with clandestine escapades that evening!"

"Indeed," Gemma mused, her brow knitting in concentration. "It indicates she was engaged in some mischief. But the devil's in the details, and I haven't the foggiest how we'll unearth Piper's secrets."

* * *

THE ROSE DINING Hall buzzed with the quiet hum of conversations, its rose and gold elegance framing the day's drama as surely as the windows framed the expanse of ocean beyond. Still nibbling on sandwiches and sipping her tea, Gemma glanced at Viv across their table.

"Would you look at that?"

Piper Vanderhall stormed into the Rose Dining Hall, her strawberry blonde locks haphazardly twisted atop her head in a messy bun, her expression souring the air with every step she took. Nina and the other chorus ladies trailed behind her like a gaggle of chattering geese.

Sitting at a table near the entrance, the women bowed their heads together, voices low with occasional bursts of emotion.

"I say," Gemma remarked. "I suddenly find myself ready to take my leave."

"Translation?" Viv stared at her.

"I'm speaking perfect English."

"Too perfect, hon," Viv looked at her over her tea cup.

Rising from her seat, Gemma gestured for Viv to join her. With a look of understanding, Viv followed. As they glided past the entryway, Nina caught their glance, offering a tentative wave. Gemma acknowledged her with a curt nod, maintaining her composed demeanor as she made her way through the main exit. Once outside, she paused and subtly leaned back, angling her head just enough to keep an eye on the table of women.

"Look at you being all eavesdroppy," Viv murmured, matching Gemma's stealth as she sidled up to her companion.

Gemma put a finger to her lips and focused on the group around the corner.

"How are we supposed to sing backup for that tramp?" one chorus lady hissed, venom laced in her voice. "Lucia is worse than Valentina ever was, now that she has no competition. For crying out loud, she wants us to do double rehearsals every day of this God-forsaken cruise."

Nina Pavlova's dark eyes darted around before settling on Piper. "She sure landed the big fish out of this deal. Do you think she knows anything about what happened to Valentina?"

"Who knows?" Piper scoffed, looking up from her phone long enough to grab a sandwich. "I bet she's been grilled just like the rest of us by that nob in security. Did he treat you like guilty until proven innocent?"

The other women murmured in agreement as Piper continued to vent.

"Just because I'm not crying my eyes out doesn't mean I shanked her," she spat out. "Valentina treated me worse than dirt. She'd call at all hours, had me washing her thongs by hand, and kicked me out whenever she pleased."

Gemma exchanged a look with Viv and leaned in further.

"Yeah," Piper went on, oblivious to the two eavesdroppers nearby, "she booted me out before midnight that night because Dirk was coming over for one of their special meetings." She rolled her eyes dramatically. "You know how they were—fought like cats and dogs one minute and then tangled up the next."

A ripple of knowing chuckles spread among the chorus girls, their sidelong glances at one another laced with shared amusement and unspoken tales.

"So, where did you go after Valentina gave you the boot?" Nina prodded.

Piper shrugged nonchalantly. "I just wandered around the ship, playing on my phone until around three or four in the morning." Her voice lowered even further as she confided in her friends. "When I returned, Valentina was passed out cold in bed—typical."

Viv's eyebrow arched toward Gemma as they digested this information silently.

"And then?" Nina pressed.

Piper frowned slightly. "I went to bed in the super comfy cot my favorite boss ever arranged for me so I could wait on her hand and foot. I was up and out by six for a Pilates class by some German chick that takes her job way too seriously." She grimaced at the memory. "By the time I got back from breakfast...well, you know."

Gemma and Viv exchanged a meaningful look once more as the women shifted their conversation away from Valentina's death.

Viv gave Gemma a covert nod, and in silent agreement, they both edged down the corridor. They paused at an expansive window, taking in the sight of the undulating ocean waves that glistened under the slowly setting sun.

"No mention of that duffel bag," Viv commented once they were sure they wouldn't be overheard.

Gemma nodded thoughtfully. "Indeed. And she certainly isn't 'crying her eyes out' over Valentina's demise." She took a moment to jot down this new revelation on their growing list—Piper's lack of alibi during critical hours made her top suspect list material.

"And kicked out just before midnight?" Viv added skeptically. "Right when Dirk supposedly arrived? Convenient timing."

"Indeed," Gemma agreed. The detail about playing on her phone could be an alibi—or a convenient cover story for those unaccounted hours when Valentina met her end.

"She seems quite bitter about Valentina," Gemma observed quietly, watching Piper laugh at something one of the chorus members said.

Viv nodded vigorously. "Bitter enough to murder?"

"That remains to be seen." Gemma pursed her lips

thoughtfully, considering motives and opportunity—a toxic brew in any murder mystery.

"Motivation? Check," Viv listed off with dramatic hand gestures. "Opportunity? Sounds like it."

"Alibi?" Gemma raised an eyebrow.

Viv shook her head. "No solid alibi from what we've heard."

They both looked back at Piper, who was now scrolling through her phone again, seemingly disconnected from the rest of the group, who continued chatting animatedly about rehearsal schedules and stage positions.

"Piper may not mourn Valentina," Gemma mused aloud, more to herself than Viv, "but she surely harbors no love lost for her late employer."

"So onto our list, she goes," Viv concluded with a firm nod.

"Lucia Rossi as well," Gemma noted, her pencil hovering before she etched a question mark beside the new diva's name. "We need to get more info on Valentina's rival and their manager, Dirk, as well."

Gemma tucked away their improvised suspect list and shook her head in amazement. She had never imagined retirement would involve piecing together such an intricate puzzle aboard a luxury cruise liner.

But there they were: two retirees drawn into intrigue over highseas homicide. With their tea behind them and their suspect list lengthening by the hour, Gemma knew this investigation was far from over—it was only deepening with each passing moment aboard this floating enclave of secrets and lies.

CHAPTER 16

*G*emma leaned on her cane, her gray eyes reflecting the fiery hues of the setting sun. Together, the two women watched in silent reverence as the sun dipped into the ocean, painting the evening sky with strokes of fuchsia, peach, violet, and yellow—a canvas that stretched endlessly before them.

The clink of fine china and the hum of idle chatter down the hall provided a soothing backdrop as they considered their next move.

"Can you believe the cruise is halfway done already?" Viv asked, radiant in her enthusiasm. "Time is flying because I am having so much fun with this 'project' of ours."

Gemma was reluctant to admit that she was enjoying the experience. A murder mystery wasn't exactly what she'd envisioned for her inaugural retirement cruise, much less playing detective with a retired Vegas showgirl who irritated, fascinated, and inspired her.

"We should seize the day, or rather the evening," Gemma peered at Viv over the rim of her glasses. "If Dirk visited

Valentina during those critical hours, regardless of his reasons, we need to learn more about him."

Viv's eyes sparkled with intrigue. "He'll be at the theater tonight for Lucia's performance."

"Two birds, one stone," Gemma mused. She sighed inwardly at the prospect of dressing up again, but she knew it was necessary for their investigation. Professionalism had always driven her to complete any task she started, and this newfound sleuthing endeavor was no exception.

"Very well," Gemma conceded, "I'll change into something suitable and meet you at the Theater."

Viv laughed heartily. "Darling, this is cruise life! Minus the murder, of course." She gestured expansively. "No cooking, no cleaning, endless entertainment, a cavalcade of interesting people, and you can drink all you like without worrying about driving!"

Gemma couldn't help but smirk at Viv's romanticizing. "Yes, well," she retorted dryly, "in the cavalcade of interesting people, you might also meet a murderer."

Viv's laughter rippled through the air, a light counter to the grim topic. "A boring murderer would be so disappointing," she quipped. With a flourish of her hand and a playful wiggle of her fingers bidding farewell, she turned and sashayed away, each step down the hallway exuding her carefree grace.

Gemma's steps were brisk as she hurried back to her room and took Buddy along the promenade deck for his walk. The Cocker-Tzu's joyous prance as they walked together brought a warm smile to her face. "You're a blessing, Buddy," she whispered, her gaze softening. "For all the lavish luxuries on this ship and the many treasures in the world, these simple moments are priceless." With a doggy smile on his little brown and black face, he seemed to say, "I love you too."

Upon returning to her quarters, Gemma approached her wardrobe with the methodical mindset of a seasoned head housekeeper. She chose a long navy blue dress that exuded tasteful elegance, complemented by sensible flats that promised comfort for the evening ahead. A small feathered fascinator hat perched neatly atop her steel gray hair, its subtle charm enhanced by a mother-of-pearl brooch—a parting gift from her employer, a token of appreciation for years of unwavering service.

Gemma slipped into the theater, the show poised to begin at any second. Viv caught her eye from the front row, her brilliant smile as illuminating as a lighthouse guiding ships through night's shroud. She was draped in a sequined turquoise outfit that shimmered with the vibrancy of a peacock's plumage, catching the glow of the overhead lights and casting playful reflections around her.

Lucia Rossi stepped into the spotlight, the theater's grandeur serving as the perfect backdrop for her captivating presence. Adorned in a floor-length black gown that hugged her silhouette, the fabric shimmered with each measured step she took. A daring plunging neckline drew eyes to the cascade of diamonds adorning her neck, each stone catching the light to send prisms dancing across the walls. Her shoulder-length jet-black hair tumbled in voluminous curls that softly caressed her heart-shaped face. With lips painted a bold blood red, and eyes that shimmered with a dark, glamorous luster, she offered the audience a smile that hinted at a secret only she was privy to. As the first haunting notes of the overture filled the air, her confident, enigmatic air promised an unforgettable performance.

"Thank you all; it's a joy to be with you again tonight," she spoke in a rich, throaty voice. "Please, enjoy the show."

"A joy?" Gemma murmured to Viv as a waiter set their

drinks down. "Quite a thing to say under these circumstances."

Lucia's rendition of "Casta Diva" swelled through the theater, her voice climbing with such clarity and power that it seemed to command the air. As she reached the aria's crescendo, the chorus girls' harmonies wove seamlessly with her melody, enriching the performance with layers of haunting resonance. The performance was spellbinding; even Gemma couldn't deny the chill that ran down her spine as Lucia hit the high notes.

During intermission, Viv leaned close to Gemma. "There he is," she whispered, nodding subtly toward Dirk, who stood by the bar, looking as impeccable but as out of place as Gemma felt.

They watched him from their vantage point—Dirk sipping a dark amber liquid from his glass while his eyes scanned the crowd with a practiced lingering gaze.

Gemma studied him intently through her glasses. There was something unnervingly calm about him amidst such turmoil—a demeanor that piqued her suspicion further.

The lights dimmed once more for Lucia's final act. As Gemma's eyes remained locked on Dirk from across the room, she pondered their next move in unraveling this tangled web aboard the Princess of Paradise. What ploy could they concoct to loosen such a man's tongue and coax out the secrets he held?

* * *

As THE FINAL note of Lucia Rossi's performance vibrated through the grand theater, a wave of applause surged from the audience. Sitting beside Viv, Gemma clapped politely, her mind not entirely on the music but instead on the investigation that had wrapped her and Viv in its coils. She was about to suggest they order another round of drinks from the waiter when Viv leaned in.

"Come on, let's go get a fresh drink," Viv suggested with a wink, nudging Gemma from her seat.

Gemma hesitated. "But we could just order from—"

"No time like the present for a little stroll," Viv interrupted, already threading her way through the crowd with Gemma in tow.

At the bar, Viv stood close to Dirk Straggler, who was engaged in his applause. She mouthed her gin and tonic order toward the bartender. As he handed her glass over, she made a clumsy gesture, and her drink cascaded down Dirk's trousers.

"Oh, my stars! I am so sorry!" Viv gasped, eyes wide as she took in the spreading stain marring the man's tailored slacks.

Dirk's face screwed up in irritation, then did a double-take, "Vivian? Vivian Carlisle? You could spill a whole bottle on me if it meant I could see you 'Turn Back Time' again."

"Dirk," Viv beamed, her trademark grin lighting up her features. "You remember my Cher number? I'm flattered."

Dirk waved away her apology. "Best show in Vegas. I'd pay top dollar to see that performance again."

Gemma settled on a barstool, lips forming a wry smile, eyes alight with appreciation of Viv's impromptu performance.

The bartender quickly handed over a replacement drink, which Viv accepted gracefully. She slid closer to Dirk, pretending to dab at his wet trousers with a napkin.

"You know," she cooed, "I've always admired how you handle your stars. Must be quite the balancing act."

Dirk accepted another whiskey from the bartender and nodded appreciatively at Viv's compliment. His face soured as he said, "Valentina was…a handful."

Viv's eyes shone with an intoxicating blend of sympathy

and curiosity as she probed further. "I can only imagine the passion in opera extends beyond the stage."

He downed his whiskey in one gulp, his jaw setting hard as memories seemed to flood back. "Passion is one word for it," Dirk said with an edge of bitterness creeping into his voice. "That first night on this damn cruise...she lured me into her room with crocodile tears. I can't believe I thought..."

His eyes flashed before he motioned the bartender for a refill.

Gemma leaned in closer, pretending to be engrossed in fixing a nonexistent run in her stockings while listening intently.

"The truth is," Dirk continued, his voice growing darker with each word, "she spent money like there was no tomorrow—furs, jewels...you name it. I had to set limits, or we'd both be sunk." He scoffed. "That night, I told her I'd set a lower limit on her cards if she didn't rein it in. Then she had the gall to threaten me—said she'd tell everyone I took advantage of her unless I increased her credit limits."

He paused to breathe deeply through his nose before continuing.

"She had tried to soften me up with that damned wine some fan had left her, then lay down the gauntlet. She knew she had me by the short hairs."

Viv patted his arm consolingly as he shook his head ruefully. "So what did you do?"

Dirk's gaze turned inward as if reliving that night's argument. "I told her what she hates to hear: no. Then, there was nothing left to stay for," he admitted quietly. "I went back to my room sometime after one and drank until I passed out."

Viv clucked sympathetically while Gemma mulled over Dirk's words.

"I woke up alone with a splitting headache. Valentina was

late for rehearsal again, only this time she actually had an excuse," he snorted as he looked into his glass. "Now she's dead, and I have no alibi and all her debts."

The revelation hung heavily between them as Dirk finished his drink.

"It looks like Valentina screwed you over in life and death," Viv remarked sympathetically.

Dirk nodded glumly, staring into the empty glass.

CHAPTER 17

irk's revelations tapered off, and into the din of
the bustling theater bar walked Piper Vanderhall;
her strawberry blonde hair a bright beacon among the dark
suits and shimmering dresses. She tapped Dirk on the shoulder, her voice a whip of urgency. "Lucia's looking for you,"
she said.

Dirk straightened his jacket with a sigh, his eyes briefly
meeting Viv's before he excused himself with a wink. "We'll
catch up again, Viv. I want to see you light up the stage one
day soon."

Once he vanished into the crowd, Gemma turned to Viv
with furrowed brows. "Do you believe him?" Viv asked as
they huddled over their untouched drinks. The clinking
glasses and applause from the theater behind them faded into
a dull murmur as they dissected Dirk's confession.

Gemma tapped her fingers on the table, her gaze distant.
"He has a motive—Valentina's threats could have ruined him,
and still could if word got out. But something doesn't sit
right." She felt like she was piecing together a jigsaw puzzle
with half the pieces missing.

"Anger and fear can drive a man to do terrible things," Viv said, swirling her drink absentmindedly.

"As can money and love," Gemma responded, her eyes scanning the room where elegantly dressed passengers mingled after the show. "One thing is certain: the wine Henri left wasn't poisoned."

Viv raised her eyebrows in shock. "You're right," she gasped. "He'd be dead as a doorknob if it had been the murder weapon."

"Indeed," Gemma agreed, the corners of her mouth turning upward in a small smile. "I do not doubt the ship's chief of security will find this detail intriguing. While he may not have earned our goodwill, Henri certainly warrants exoneration."

Turning, Gemma felt the room begin to sway subtly beneath her. The chatter around them echoed in a cavernous space, and she gripped the bar's edge tighter.

Oh no, not now, she pleaded silently, squeezing her eyes shut as she sought solace in a quick, desperate prayer.

"Gemma? You're white as a ghost," Viv observed with concern etched on her face.

With an abrupt motion, Gemma tried to stand but was met with a treacherous rush of vertigo forcing her back down into her seat. She pressed a hand to her forehead and closed her eyes briefly, waiting for the spinning sensation to pass.

"No exercise classes tomorrow," she murmured, opening her eyes to find Viv peering at her with worry. "I'll take Bonnie's advice and stick to low-impact walking."

Viv frowned, sliding closer. "What happened just now? You look like you're about to keel over."

"It's nothing," Gemma said as she attempted another smile that didn't quite reach her eyes. "A bit of rest should set me straight."

"Alright," Viv said, her eyes skeptical. "But I'm walking you back to your room."

Despite Gemma's protests, Viv linked arms with her and guided her out of the bar and back towards her cabin. The walk seemed longer than usual; every step was measured, careful not to aggravate Gemma's condition.

Inside Gemma's cabin, Buddy greeted them with excited barks that quickly turned into concerned whines as he sensed his owner's distress. With an unexpected gentleness, Viv helped Gemma settle onto her bed as Buddy curled up protectively at her feet.

"You mustn't fuss over me like this," Gemma said with an embarrassed grimace. "I'm—I'll be fine."

Viv perched on the edge of the bed, looking at Gemma appraisingly. "You gonna tell me what's going on, hon?"

The question hung in the air like a heavy curtain ready to fall at the end of a performance. For years, Gemma had wrapped herself in layers of self-reliance and privacy—a shield against pity or unwelcome assistance. No one ever knew her private suffering. Yet here was Viv—a woman she'd known for barely a few days—peeling back those layers, much to Gemma's consternation.

Was it indeed such a terrible prospect? To let her guard down, if only momentarily?

Gemma sighed heavily. "Chronic vertigo has been my shadow for years. A succession of childhood earaches laid the groundwork, and then a dreadful infection a decade past wreaked havoc on my inner ear. While my hearing isn't impaired, the spells come. They're unpredictable, ranging from mild to debilitating. Hence, the cane—it's not just an accessory, it's a necessity."

She braced herself for what she thought would be Viv's overbearing concern or worse—pity.

Instead, Viv offered a warm smile that reached to her

green eyes. "Thank you for trusting me enough to tell me," she said softly. "You're strong and independent—and I admire that about you—but everyone needs help sometimes."

Her words were like a balm on an old wound—soothing yet unexpectedly poignant.

"I don't want this condition to define me," Gemma confessed quietly.

"It doesn't," Viv assured her firmly. "It's just one part of who you are—a brilliant, mature woman solving a murder mystery on her first cruise!"

Gemma chuckled despite herself, and Buddy thumped his tail as his mistress's mood lightened.

"Get some rest now," Viv said as she stood up from the bed and moved towards the door. "We'll continue our little project tomorrow if you're ready. Fernando and I will pop by in the morning, okay?"

With a nod, Gemma tried to force down the flush of embarrassment, warming her cheeks. Viv, meanwhile, glided across the room with the ease of a dancer, reaching for the door handle.

Buddy watched Viv leave before returning to Gemma, offering his silent support as she lay back against her pillows. The soft sounds of waves lapping against the ship's hull played through their porthole—a lullaby coaxing them both towards sleep.

As darkness settled in around them and silence enveloped the room save for Buddy's rhythmic breathing beside her bed, Gemma realized how this friendship had caught her off guard—an unexpected twist in what she expected would be a solitary trip. It seemed not all surprises on this cruise were unwelcome after all.

* * *

GEMMA NESTLED under the covers in the quiet darkness of her cabin, the rhythmic thrum of the ship's engines below weaving its way through the silence, coaxing her toward slumber. Buddy nestled beside her, his soulful brown eyes gazing up in loyal concern. As she waited for sleep, she ran her fingers through his fur, indulging in the rhythmic motion as she pondered the day's revelations.

"Quite the conundrum we've landed in, eh Buddy?" she murmured, her fingers tracing gentle circles on his belly. His tail responded with a contented thump against the soft comforter. "The list of suspects has only grown longer, yet the real culprit remains as elusive as ever."

She listed their suspects aloud, each name punctuated by a soft pat on Buddy's belly.

"Piper," she started. "She omitted telling the other chorus members about that duffel bag. What was she hiding? Anger towards Valentina is clear, but is it enough for murder? And her alibi is non-existent."

Buddy tilted his head as if to offer sympathy for Piper's predicament, or perhaps to angle for more belly rubs.

"Then there's Dirk," Gemma continued, her tone growing heavier. "He had more reasons than one to want Valentina silent: the threat to expose him, the financial ruin she dragged him into… But again, no witnesses, no alibi."

Buddy let out a soft whine. It was as though he understood the gravity of their situation—or maybe he sensed Gemma's deepening concern.

"And Henri," she sighed. "The sommelier with a penchant for too much wine and unrequited love. Seen leaving a present at Valentina's door that very night, and then he lied about it." Gemma shook her head disapprovingly. "His motive might be obsession, but that doesn't make a murderer…or does it?

"Then there is Lucia Rossi," Gemma mused, her voice

tinged with suspicion. "Valentina's archrival who slid into the spotlight with such grace, it was as if she'd been waiting in the wings."

Buddy rolled onto his back, fully exposing his belly in a silent plea for more attention. As Gemma obliged, her thoughts wandered from suspects and motives to self-doubt.

"Grimshaw may be as personable as a barnacle," she confided to Buddy, "but he isn't entirely wrong. Meg has been cleared—thanks to Viv—and perhaps this is where our involvement should end."

Buddy huffed softly as if in disagreement or adjusting to a more comfortable position.

"I'm not Father Brown," Gemma admitted with a tinge of sadness. "This isn't just a story from one of my books where everything tidies up tickety boo by the final chapter." She gazed down at Buddy with a weariness that went beyond physical ailments. "I'm sore; my stomach has been staging its mutiny since day one, and this cruise was supposed to be about relaxation."

Her voice trailed off into the quiet of her cabin. Buddy licked her hand gently—a simple gesture that spoke volumes of his empathy.

Gemma leaned back against her pillows and stroked Buddy's fur as she mulled over Grimshaw's words. She had intended to retire in peace—not chase shadows and secrets on the high seas with a woman who lived life louder than a brass band.

The soft patter of rain drew Gemma's gaze toward the window. The dark ocean sky beyond mirrored her inner tumult—waves of doubt crashing against the steadfast desire to see justice served.

Viv seemed invigorated by their amateur investigation—a Vegas showgirl dazzling under the spotlight once more—while Gemma felt every bit her age and then some.

Was it indeed her place to meddle further? Or should she leave this mystery in Grimshaw's capable—if somewhat ham-fisted—hands?

She closed her eyes against these thoughts, hoping sleep would grant her clarity. But even as slumber tugged at her consciousness, one thought lingered stubbornly: if she abandoned this puzzle now, would it haunt her for the rest of her days?

CHAPTER 18

*G*emma awoke to the gentle swaying of the ship and Buddy's soft snoring at the foot of her bed. Sitting up, she felt rejuvenated. The disorienting vertigo that had gripped her the evening before had dissipated like fog at sunrise. All that remained were her lingering self-doubts.

She arose slowly and wrapped a soft gray robe around herself. Padding to the kettle, she began preparations for a perfectly brewed cup of tea. As the water boiled, her mind bubbled with doubts from the night before. Was it indeed her place to meddle in this mystery? Was she cut from the same cloth as Father Brown or was she fooling herself to think she had any of his skill in real life? Would her vertigo crop up at the worst possible time, rendering her useless, becoming an impediment when this unofficial investigation might matter most?

Pressing her lips together, Gemma sighed and sat in her armchair with her doubts and fears. Looking out the port-hole at the slowly clearing gray sky outside, Gemma sipped her tea. Buddy stirred from his slumber, let out a broad yawn that showcased his small white teeth, and trotted over to Gemma, his tail picking up momentum in a cheerful wag.

"I say," Gemma smiled and rubbed his head. "It must be lovely to sleep in and wake up with not a care in the world."

Draining her cup of its final tepid dregs, Gemma rose. "This simply will not do," she declared to the empty room. "I made a vow to share my observations and insights with Viv, and that's precisely what I'll do...for what it's worth. For now, it's high time for your walk, my boy."

Gemma stood, swiftly pulling the sheets tight and tucking the corners with the precise movements honed from years of meticulous housekeeping. She donned a tasteful blouse paired with a skirt that fell just below the knee and her reliable, comfortable shoes.

Buddy's leash in hand, she opened the door to find Vivian Carlisle already waiting outside, Fernando in tow.

"Good morning," Viv singsonged. "It's good to see you up and at 'em after our eventful night."

"Eventful, indeed," Gemma harrumped. "I can't tell if that's kindness or your wit showing."

"A dash of each," Viv replied with a grin, her eyes twinkling with mischief. "We hit a gold mine of information with Dirk, don't you think?"

"We did," Gemma tilted her head. "I'll have to remember to spill a drink on an unsuspecting man in the future when I need information."

Gemma appreciated Viv's discretion, starkly contrasting from the smothering concern she had anticipated following last night's escapade. There was no fawning, no intrusive queries—just the sort of respect for her privacy that Gemma held dear.

As the two women walked toward the elevators, Gemma looked at Viv's toy Chihuahua and bit her lip to swallow the laugh threatening to escape. Fernando was decked out in a tiny blue jogging suit that matched Viv's vibrant tracksuit. His hood pulled up over his pointy ears, he looked up at Gemma and Buddy with what could only be described as disdain before giving a begrudging sniff in Buddy's direction. Buddy's tail wagged furiously, his tongue lolling out in delight at even this tiny acknowledgment from Fernando.

Soon seated at a rooftop cafe table with a panoramic view of the endless ocean, they ordered their breakfast—Viv opting for fruit, granola, and orange juice, while Gemma opted for the comfort of poached eggs on toast with tea. While they awaited their breakfast, the nagging uncertainties that plagued Gemma's thoughts in the quiet hours resurfaced, as sudden and disorienting as her sporadic vertigo.

A flicker of hope mingled with apprehension in her heart: opening up to Viv hadn't resulted in overbearing concern or crippling embarrassment. Maybe extending herself further wouldn't be so perilous after all?

With a slight cough to steady her nerves, Gemma found her voice. "I've never been one for...well, new things," she admitted her finger absentmindedly following the delicate curve of her teacup's rim. "Managing an entire housekeeping staff, making a bed to military precision—that's my comfort zone. Yet, I'm questioning my competence in handling our current endeavor."

The server set down their drinks, and Viv, her eyes alight with understanding, leaned closer across the table. "Honey, I've wrestled with my share of uncertainties. Three ex-husbands will teach you a thing or two. But it's just those trials that showed me what I was made of. You've got more strength than you give yourself credit for. We can stop all this if you want, but if you're willing, we should keep going. We've uncovered so much already, just us two clever cats working our way through the ship, using our natural charms and hidden talents."

"The lady doth protest too much, methinks," Gemma quipped. "Natural charm is your department, Viv, dear. I'll claim the hidden talents if you please." Her eyes, usually sharp and assessing, twinkled with a rare hint of playfulness behind wire-rimmed glasses.

A laugh escaped Viv as she lifted her glass of orange juice high, acknowledging the comment with an approving tilt.

Sensing the softer mood at the table, Buddy edged closer to Fernando, who lay curled beside Viv. The little Chihuahua's gaze was haughty, but when Buddy's nose nudged his behind, a begrudging sniff was exchanged between them—a tacit canine truce.

Gemma's bemused smile lingered as she watched the dogs, then with a decisive turn, she retrieved a folded sheet from her purse. Unfolding it carefully, she spread it across the table, the meticulous list of names written in her precise script.

"First things first, let's get organized," Gemma intoned, nudging her glasses up her nose. "Our suspects' list is grow-ing, yet we're missing pieces of this puzzle."

Viv nodded. "Agreed. We know Dirk had both motive and opportunity, Henri is potentially the 'biggest fan' and had access to Valentina's quarters, but the wine wasn't poisoned —he could have used another method to be fair, and Piper... well, Piper's a mystery with her midnight duffel bag escapade."

"And then there's Lucia," Gemma added thoughtfully. "She benefits most visibly from Valentina's death—stepping into the spotlight without so much as a hitch in her step."

They paused as breakfast arrived, and Gemma sipped her tea while pondering their next move. "We should learn more about Piper's movements and what was in that duffel bag. As for Lucia—"

"—We need to know if she had any contact with Valentina

before it happened," Viv finished for her, swirling her spoon through her granola.

"Exactly." Gemma nodded and made a note on her list.

As they discussed their plan of action, Viv whipped out her phone with a magician's flourish, revealing a trick. Her fingers danced across the screen as she muttered about checking social media for clues.

Gemma couldn't help but frown at the device. "You put too much faith in that thing," she chided gently. "There's no substitute for traditional methods—observation, interviews, deduction."

Viv chuckled without looking up from her screen. "And you're so set in your old ways you'd probably try to solve this case with nothing but a magnifying glass and your intuition. Though that eavesdropping stunt you pulled yesterday was impressive."

Gemma offered a nod of affirmation. "The classics never go out of style," she asserted with a hint of pride. "They demand patience and a sharp eye—qualities, I'm afraid, that seem scarce in an era where everyone's eyes are perpetually fixed to their screens."

Viv's eyes twinkled as she continued tapping away at her phone. "And yet here I am, about to uncover what your 'keen eye' may have missed because I can access information you can't." She squinted at the screen and grumbled about the ship's spotty Wi-Fi.

Gemma clucked disapprovingly. "That's precisely my point; you rely on technology that may fail you when you need it most." She leaned forward, warming to her subject. "In my day, we learned to rely on ourselves—our wits were our Wi-Fi."

Viv laughed outright now. "Oh, Gemma, you have such a way with words. Seriously though, sometimes we need all the help we can get—even if it comes from this wired-up world." Viv's eyes narrowed as she leaned in, her voice dropping to an excited whisper. "Oh, ho, ho, what have we here?"

Gemma's curiosity piqued, and she edged closer, her skepticism momentarily forgotten. "What is it?" she inquired, unable to mask the intrigue in her voice.

"Naughty girl," Viv announced with a smirk, her finger rhythmically drumming on the screen as if to punctuate the revelation. She then kicked back in her chair, satisfaction radiating like heat from the pavement on a summer day. "I know *exactly* what Piper was up to the other night."

CHAPTER 19

*V*iv's eyes danced with the kind of mischief that Gemma had come to associate with the imminent unraveling of another piece of their mystery. The retired showgirl tapped away at her phone with a manicured nail, smiling with satisfaction.

"Well, will you tell me what you found, or will I have to wait until my tea is quite cold?" Gemma inquired, peering over the rim of her spectacles as she took a delicate sip of her Earl Grey.

"Hold your horses. This will be worthwhile. These kids make it too easy," Viv scoffed, tilting the screen towards Gemma. "Look what Piper was up to the other night."

Gemma leaned in, squinting at images of Piper illuminated on the device. "Since when is vanity considered news? The young are forever snapping pictures of themselves."

Viv smirked, scrolling through an album of selfies. "It's not the selfies that are naughty; it's what she's wearing in them."

"Selfies," Gemma furrowed her brow in confusion. "What newfangled word is this?"

"For someone who just said newfangled, I can understand you could use a modern dictionary."

"Oxford English Dictionary only for me, my dear Vivian. Now, what is this word, and what am I looking at on this screen?"

"A selfie, darling, is a photograph that one takes of oneself," Viv explained, her voice dripping with patience. "Usually with a smartphone. It's the modern way of capturing a moment without bothering anyone else for assistance."

Gemma gave the concept a skeptical once-over. "Sounds like a recipe for narcissism."

Viv laughed. "Perhaps, but in our case, it's the perfect recipe for sleuthing. Look at these." She gestured at the screen again, where Piper pouted and preened.

"And what exactly am I supposed to be looking at?" Gemma adjusted her glasses and peered closer.

Viv swiped the screen to enlarge Piper's photos, each frame showcasing the young woman draped dramatically in sumptuous furs, puckering her lips at the camera. Around her neck hung an assortment of jewels, their facets catching the light, glittering even in the harsh glare of the camera's flash.

"I'd be willing to bet all my chips at the casino that those aren't her furs or jewels. What do you think?"

"Looks like a safe bet," Gemma nodded.

Viv's finger flicked across the screen with practiced ease, each swipe unveiling more of Piper's midnight escapades—a series of poses akin to a clandestine photo shoot set against the backdrop of the ship's opulence.

"Stop there," Gemma interjected, her excitement palpable. She reached out with a tentative hand. "May I have a look?"

Viv handed her phone over with an amused smile. Gemma initially tapped her finger at the screen uncertainly, then soon found the right pressure point to slide the photos.

"Here," Gemma gestured to Viv, "Notice anything?"

Viv leaned closer, her eyes narrowing as she scrutinized the image. Piper had struck a flamboyant pose, fingers splayed in a peace sign. The black fur coat hung off her shoulders, unabashedly open to showcase the glinting silver necklace beneath—a cascade of diamonds punctuated by a bold emerald pendant at its heart.

Gemma's smile held a triumphant edge. "Strikingly similar to Valentina's, wouldn't you agree?" She tilted her head, eyeing the photo with a jeweler's precision. "The self-same piece she donned for her debut...and final performance."

"You're right," Viv said. "Remember the duffel bag Bonnie saw? What if it was filled with loot from Valentina's collection?"

"It seems Ms. Vanderhall has been helping herself to more than just a paycheck," Gemma murmured. "Piper was certainly bitter about being cast out into the night by Valentina. She had spoken with venom about sleeping on a cot in Valentina's shadow, always at her beck and call."

Viv nodded. "Look at the timestamp."

Gemma squinted and saw the time on the photos tell their own story that contradicted Piper's narrative. "She claimed to wander after being sent away by Valentina, but these publicly available photos suggest a different story."

"Not publicly," Viv corrected with a wag of her finger. "She posted these privately, but nothing escapes the internet once it's out there."

Gemma pondered this new information. "How does one post something 'privately'?"

Viv leaned in conspiratorially. "It's all about settings and knowing who can see what you share. It's meant for friends' eyes only—but there are ways around that if you're savvy enough."

"And I take it you are quite savvy," Gemma said, a small smile curving her lips.

Viv's smile widened, her eyes twinkling with mischief. "Honeybun, I've got pals peppered across the digital realm— from young whippersnappers to wrinkly old-timers—who've shared their cyber secrets with me," she chuckled, amusement dancing in her voice. Fingers deftly swiping across her phone, she perused a few more snapshots, then, with a dramatic tap, locked her device and tucked it into her handbag, her movements as theatrical as ever.

Gemma weighed their options, her gaze steady. "We could confront Piper directly," she proposed. "Offer her the opportunity to spill the tea before Grimshaw uncovers this himself."

"Or we let our dear security chief find his clues," Viv suggested with a wry grin. "He was quite adamant we stay out of it, after all. I have every intention of docking in New York, not Iceland."

"Indeed," Gemma concurred with a slight nod. "What he doesn't know won't hurt him. However, what Piper is hiding could hurt her."

Viv caught Gemma's attention across the breakfast table with a slight tilt of her glass. "Speak of the angel," she said, a sly note in her voice as she gestured subtly. "Look!"

As the morning sun crept higher in the sky, Gemma spotted Piper. The younger woman jogged along the ship's uppermost deck, her silhouette sharpened against the burgeoning day. Her aviators glinted in the sunlight as she bounced in her thigh-high shorts, earbuds sealing her off from anything beyond the thrum of her private soundtrack.

Or inquiries she's keen to avoid, Gemma mused.

"Miss Vanderhall!" Gemma's voice cut through the sea breeze with an assertive edge, reminiscent of her days directing a staff of maids whose bed corners weren't perfectly square.

Piper skidded to a halt, plucking an earbud from her ear, her brow furrowed in confusion at the sight of the two older women. She looked over her sunglasses from Gemma to Viv and back again. "Did—did you call me?"

"May we have a word?"

Piper nodded warily and sat at their table. Without delay, Viv slid her phone across the table with the most damning image displayed onscreen.

Piper's mouth opened as she stared at the photos, her expression a cocktail of shock and embarrassment. "Where did you... How did you find these?" she stammered.

Gemma leaned in, a severe note underscoring her words. "If we've uncovered these images, it's only a matter of time before ship security does as well. It might be in your best interest to confide in us. We're here to listen, should you choose to speak."

Gemma watched as Piper's shoulders slumped under the weight of her confession. "I—I was just so angry with Valentina," she admitted, looking down at her feet. Piper's voice quivered with pent-up frustration, her eyes flashing with the indignity of it all. "She treated me like I was dirt under her stilettos. Piper, clean my clothes. Piper, three coats on my nails. Piper, make sure it's crushed ice in the glass, not cubed!"

Viv leaned against the table as Piper vented all of her indignities—the late-night demands, the menial tasks that went far beyond what any personal assistant should endure.

"That night," Piper's voice broke, the words tumbling out

as raw emotion swelled within her. "When she kicked me out, something inside me just broke. I don't know what got into me. The moment Valentina disappeared into the bathroom, I threw some stuff into a bag and then let off steam out on deck. It was just props, you know? Nothing serious. I was just having some fun since I literally had nothing else to do."

Gemma observed Piper's face closely, looking for any sign of deceit. But she only saw a young woman driven to foolishness by frustration and exhaustion.

"I swear," Piper said earnestly, meeting Gemma's gaze directly now, "I returned everything after my little photo shoot. I thought Valentina was asleep when I got back."

Viv shot a knowing look toward Gemma, whose lips had formed a thin, resolute line.

Piper's eyes brimmed with tears as she pleaded for their guidance. "What do I do? I should have told the truth, but if Lucia finds out about this, I'll be out of a job as soon as we hit New York. It's not like I did anything wrong. I didn't kill her, I swear."

Gemma placed a reassuring hand on Piper's shoulder. "Come clean," she advised firmly. "No one will press charges over this bit of mischief."

Piper nodded slowly, absorbing Gemma's words. Her face conveyed a medley of relief and fear—a young life poised on the edge of change.

"You have an alibi," Viv chimed in supportively. "Use it, hon; it's not worth the risk."

Gemma could see Piper wrestling with the notion of revealing all to Grimshaw—

"I'll probably get fired," Piper said gloomily.

"It's better than being wrongly accused of murder," Gemma replied sagely.

Piper sighed heavily and looked across the vast ocean

surrounding the trio. With one last glance at Gemma and Viv, Piper walked away.

"Do you think she'll come clean?" Viv asked.

"It's in her hands now," Gemma replied solemnly. "Those selfies will either be her downfall or her salvation."

CHAPTER 20

*A*s Piper disappeared, Peggy Swift strode confidently onto the deck. She was the epitome of cruise casual in her crisp white shorts, a polo shirt that hugged her long, lean frame, and a visor that shielded her keen eyes from the sun's glare.

"Ladies and gentlemen," Peggy's cheery voice boomed, amplified by the handheld megaphone she raised to her lips. "I'm thrilled to announce a special surprise!" Her announcement carried across the deck, sparking excitement among the passengers.

Gemma shuddered as she imagined another round of shuffleboard or worse—a session with Bonnie "Make It Hertz."

"Lucia Rossi has graciously offered to brighten everyone's day with a complimentary vocal lesson in the Jade Conference Room starting in twenty minutes!"

Viv scoffed beside her. "Vocal lessons? As if I need any help hitting the high notes."

"It might be our chance to get closer to Lucia and gather some information," Gemma suggested, glancing at her watch.

Time is of the essence. "Shall we drop off the dogs and investigate?"

"Fine," Viv sighed, "But this better be worth it. I'd rather square off with Bonnie Hertz on the shuffleboard court than listen to Lucia brag. Her, teach me how to sing? Please."

They parted ways momentarily to ensure Buddy and Fernando were comfortable before dashing towards the Jade Conference Room. They slipped through the door just as it was about to close.

Taking their seats at the back of the room, Gemma spotted Nina and the other chorus members sitting directly in front of them.

"I'm surprised to see you here," Gemma leaned forward and greeted the younger women. "Surely you don't need vocal lessons?"

Nina turned and whispered back conspiratorially, "Dirk insisted we attend. He wants us to learn Lucia's style quickly for more polished performances. Last night was good, but he wants perfection."

Gemma sat back, digesting this new piece of information. It painted Dirk in a desperate light, needing Lucia to shine where Valentina could no longer hold the spotlight.

Nina continued in a low voice, her eyes darting around as if afraid of being overheard. "With Valentina gone and his money troubles, he needs Lucia to be his new star. We'll do it for him, but not for her."

Viv edged closer to Gemma. "Dirk's already juggling more scandals than a circus act. Imagine throwing a murder charge into the mix."

Gemma's slow nod was contemplative, the gears visibly turning behind her steel gray eyes. "Or, what if this was his game plan from the start? Lucia was the understudy, ready to step into the spotlight." She leaned on her cane, lowering her voice to match Viv's conspiratorial tone. "Valentina's threat

to expose him could have pushed him over the edge. We mustn't rule out that he might have resorted to permanent measures to protect his reputation."

Viv's eyebrow arched skeptically, but she kept her musings to herself as Lucia Rossi, poised like a queen ascending her throne, swept in amidst a flutter of excited whispers. Gemma watched as she made her grand entrance dressed in a flowing white sundress, glittering bracelets jangling on her arms, and the sweep of her black hair trailing like the train of a royal gown.

Lucia confidently strode to the front of the Jade Conference Room, and with a poised elegance, she faced her audience, signaling the start of her session.

She addressed the room, her slender fingers resting lightly against her chest. "Ladies and gentlemen," she breathed, her eyes shimmering, "I am delighted to share the gift of song with you."

Viv's derisive snort sliced through the silence, abruptly interrupting Lucia's elegant introduction. A fleeting look of annoyance flitted across the opera singer's features before she shot a scathing look toward the culprit. From her peripheral view, Gemma observed the scene with a blend of irritation and amusement as Viv theatrically signaled her contrition, clasping her throat and issuing a soft, apologetic cough.

Leaning back in her chair, Gemma fixed her glasses as she braced for what she expected to be an unbearable session with yet another self-absorbed diva. Her patience for such characters on land and sea had worn thin long ago.

Lucia's boasts of standing ovations and encores in grand European theaters reverberated off the Jade Conference Room's walls. Viv pretended to delve into her handbag with barely concealed boredom. Her fingers closed around her lipstick; she traced her lips with the color, movements slow

and meticulous as if performing a ritual. Gemma watched, amusement flickering in her eyes, as Viv pulled out a hand cream tube, squeezing a dollop into her palm. She slathered it on in a conspicuous display of indifference. Finally, Viv punctuated the monologue with a resounding clap, her well-moisturized palms striking each other once, sharply. Lucia shot her a look of pure venom.

"For the love of Pavarotti, I'm dying of boredom over here," Viv hissed. Lucia, smiling widely, directed the motley assembly—a mix of gray-haired retirees, childless duos, and distinctly unenthused chorus ladies—through a series of rudimentary vocal exercises. Viv's eyes glinted with roguish delight, her voice scaling the octaves with theatrical flair. Much to Gemma's amusement, each note she belted out was more ostentatious and showy than its predecessor.

The moment Lucia signaled the end of the lesson, Nina and the other chorus girls bolted for the door like prisoners released from their chains. Their mutterings echoed Gemma's thoughts precisely: this had been nothing but a glorified ego trip for Lucia.

Gemma nudged Viv with her elbow. "Let's get an autograph," she whispered conspiratorially.

"Seriously?" Viv bemoaned. "Haven't I suffered enough?"

"We may pry some information out of her for our trouble."

Grumbling, Viv joined Gemma as they queued up behind a smattering of enthusiastic fans and waited their turn. As they edged closer to Lucia, Gemma felt a tinge of excitement and apprehension at their ruse. Was this a fool's errand, Gemma wondered. What did she think would happen other than a vain woman signing a slip of paper for vanity's sake?

When they finally reached the front, Viv transformed before Gemma's eyes into a fawning sycophant worthy of Oscar praise.

"Oh, Ms. Rossi," Viv gushed, her voice dripping with exaggerated adulation as she fluttered her eyelashes in an over-the-top display of adoration. "Last evening's performance was simply divine. You embodied the music, the passion—a veritable reincarnation of Maria Callas herself."

"You're too kind," a subtle smile played at the edges of Lucia's mouth, a faint indication of satisfied amusement. "One does her best to honor the greats."

Leaning in, Viv conspiratorially lowered her voice. "I can't say I'm cut up about Valentina, between you and me. In truth, your brilliance eclipses her own by such a wide margin it's as if the heavens themselves have orchestrated this change of guard."

Lucia's response was a smug smile that stretched across her face like a cat who had caught the canary. She leaned close to Viv as if they were old confidants sharing secrets over tea.

"Thank you, darling," Lucia purred as she scribbled on a glossy photo of herself in a dramatic pose. "It's fans like you who make it all worthwhile." She handed the photograph to Viv with a flourish. Sighing, Viv held it to her chest as their turn ended.

Gemma fought to maintain a neutral expression, half expecting Viv to curtsy.

As they walked from the autograph table, all fawning pretenses fell from Viv's face. Stepping into the hallway, Viv paused.

"I'm sorry, hon. All we got was this stupid thing," Viv apologized, waving the paper.

Gemma cocked an eyebrow, scrutinizing the glossy portrait of Lucia. "What's the dedication?" she inquired, nodding toward the autograph.

With a flick of her wrist, Viv angled the headshot for better viewing.

Hell hath no fury...

xx

Lucia Rossi

Gemma's heart skipped a beat as she read the message over Viv's shoulder. Was this mere bravado or something more sinister? They exchanged a glance loaded with unspoken questions.

Gemma turned to Viv. "Do you reckon—"

Viv's eager nod sliced through Gemma's words. "You better believe it," she confirmed with urgency. "This means something, and we had better hurry up to find out what."

emma shifted her weight onto the sturdy cane, her toe tapping a steady beat against the gleaming wooden deck of the Princess, a ship that had transformed into a maze, brimming with hushed whispers and hidden truths. Beside her, Viv's eyes grew round with intrigue, her fingers tightening instinctively around the edges of the autographed photo, a potential key to unraveling the mystery at hand.

"Hell hath no fury," Viv read aloud once more, her voice tinged with excitement. "Sounds like something out of a movie, doesn't it?"

"It's from a play, in fact," Gemma corrected, pushing her glasses up the bridge of her nose. "The Mourning Bride by William Congreve. 'Hell hath no fury like a woman scorned.' It's been misquoted over time, but the essence remains—a woman wronged can be exceptionally vengeful."

Viv arched an eyebrow. "And you think our dear Ms. Rossi is trying to tell us something with this little dedication?"

"Perhaps," Gemma pondered, her steel gray eyes

narrowing in thought as possibilities danced like shadows across her mind. "Shall we take a turn around the deck to mull over what this could imply?"

"Let's do it," Viv replied eagerly, her voice carrying the thrill of impending discovery. She slipped her arm through Gemma's, offering support as much as seeking camaraderie. Momentarily taken aback, Gemma glanced at the vivacious woman's arm linked with hers. Yet, instead of recoiling from the intrusion into her personal bubble, she felt an unexpected comfort in the gesture.

Linked at the elbow, the two women paced the ship's wraparound walkway, surrounded by the ocean's boundless canvas. The Princess of Paradise sliced through the water at a smooth pace. The vast expanse of blue stretched in all directions, cradling the vessel's sleek hull, painted in bold strokes of black and red. The ship cleaved through the undulating waves, its course set firmly toward West across the Atlantic.

Gemma allowed herself a fleeting look at the breathtaking vista, her thoughts sprinting from one hypothesis to the next as if leafing through the chapters of a beloved and dog-eared detective tome.

"So, what do you think it means?" Viv broke the pensive silence enveloping them. They stopped at the bow, where the ship's sharp prow seemed to slice the horizon in two. Leaning on the cool metal railing, they peered into the ocean's abyss, its surface a glassy expanse melding seamlessly with the sky.

"It could mean many things," Gemma mused. "We must consider every angle. For instance, could Lucia have had an affection for Dirk? Maybe she was spurned by him and, in her rage, sought to eliminate Valentina."

Viv pondered this, tapping a finger against her lips. "Or perhaps it was professional jealousy? Valentina could have scorned Lucia's talents, pushing her to a deadly breaking point."

"Then there's Dirk," Gemma added thoughtfully. "Could he have been less than truthful? If he forced himself on Valentina and she was the scorned woman who threatened exposure…"

"Murder would be his cover-up," Viv finished, a shiver running down her spine despite the warmth of the sun above them. "Maybe Lucia knows something about Dirk and Valentina she doesn't want to reveal because Dirk serves a purpose in her career ambitions?"

They continued to walk in contemplative silence.

"If Dirk was telling the truth, and he did go to her room only to be ambushed by her demands for more money," Gemma posited, "she could have felt 'scorned' by his refusal to indulge her and… well, hell hath no fury indeed."

"Those are all possible explanations," Viv remarked. "But none takes us closer to unraveling the truth. Lucia could be the scorned woman, Valentina, or I don't know. She's just super dramatic, and it means nothing at all, and we are totally overthinking it."

Gemma nodded. Their conversation had turned into a whirlwind of conjecture, each hypothesis as plausible as it was distressing. The more they discussed, the more their excitement morphed into frustration; they were tangled in a web of what-ifs with no clear thread to follow.

Gemma halted abruptly. "Let's pause for a cuppa and a little nibble in my cabin," she suggested. "We can call for some crumpets. A moment of calm might help us think more clearly."

"I like the way you think," Viv concurred with a grin, her green eyes twinkling. "But first, let's swing by and scoop up my pint-sized sidekick. Fernando's been cooped up too long —he needs his walkies."

They made their way to Viv's cabin two levels up from Gemma's, Viv's high heels thumping on the carpet in a muted rhythm that matched the faint tremor of the ship's engines. At her door, Viv cooed and fussed over Fernando, who emerged in a miniature sailor outfit that mirrored the crisp whites worn by the crew. He barked his greetings before scampering around their feet, a diminutive guardian ready to join their investigation.

Accompanied by Fernando's eager prance, they proceeded to Gemma's quarters. The promenade deck had thinned out, its earlier throngs dispersed as the midday attractions—the sumptuous lunch spreads and a myriad of shipboard events—lured guests into the expansive interior of the vessel.

Nearing Gemma's quarters, a strip of white peeked from the door's edge, an anomaly against the ship's meticulous standards. It clung to the frame, an unexpected oddity that beckoned closer inspection in a setting where even minor disarray was a rarity.

Gemma's fingers brushed against the unexpected note, curiosity piqued. "What's this?" she inquired, pinching the corner of the paper and drawing it free from its snug position.

Viv chuckled, eyes twinkling with mischief as she cradled Fernando closer. "Maybe you have a secret admirer," she suggested, planting a smooch on the Chihuahua's head. Fernando responded with a slight, contented shimmy, seeming to accept the affection as his due.

With a dismissive shake of her head, Gemma scoffed lightly. "I told you, Buddy is all the love I need in my life," she stated matter-of-factly, her voice softening as she acknowl-edged the familiar sounds of her Cocker-Tzu, eagerly awaiting her return on the other side of the door. The thump of his tail and gentle whines brought a rare, warm smile to her lips.

Unfolding the note revealed crudely cut-out letters arranged in a threatening message: "Mind your own business, or you and blondie will be sleeping with the fishes."

The stark words were a slap across Gemma's face, cold and unyielding. A shudder ran through her at the implications—someone was watching them closely enough to know their meddling and Viv's distinctive presence.

Viv leaned over to read the message, her lips forming a tight line, "What the—blondie?" she said with an edge to her voice that belied her usual flamboyance.

Gemma turned over the note in her hands. The threat was clear: whoever crafted this message wanted them to fear for their safety. Someone wanted them to stop investigating.

Who harbored such a malevolent wish for their silence? To what lengths would they go to ensure it? Gemma pressed her lips into a determined line, a futile attempt to steady her trembling hand, while her gaze remained fixed on the chilling words, 'sleeping with the fishes,' the threat resonating with a grim echo in the confines of her mind.

In stark black ink, it was there—their potential fate spelled out with grim finality. That was the length to which someone was prepared to go.

CHAPTER 22

The door to Gemma's cabin clicked shut behind them, the threatening note clutched in her hand like a venomous snake. Her heart raced, yet the plush carpet seemed to swallow their footsteps and the urgency that accompanied them. Gemma moved towards the kettle, setting it on with a practiced wrist flick. Buddy padded over, pressing his warm body against her leg, while Fernando sniffed around the room suspiciously.

Viv collapsed into the plush armchair, sheen gone from her usually sparkling demeanor. "Do we need to tell someone about this?" Her green eyes flickered to the menacing message.

Gemma passed Viv a steaming cup, cradling her own as if to draw comfort from its heat. "We ought to," she acknowledged with a sigh. "This is real life, not a game of Clue. Valentina's been murdered, and with this threat…" Her voice trailed off, leaving the weight of unsaid fears to settle around them.

Viv cracked a half-hearted smile. "Well, we're too far West now. Grimshaw can't drop us off in Iceland."

Curls of steam arose from their cups as they sipped their tea silently before Gemma spoke again. "Who do you think is behind this? Could it be Piper? Or Lucia? Henri?" She paused before reluctantly adding, "Dirk? Someone else entirely we haven't even considered?"

Viv's smile had faded entirely now. "I don't know," she admitted. "But whoever it is, they're not joking around."

"Nor did I think we were, not entirely," Gemma reclined slightly, a furrow of concern etching her brow. "Why are you doing this, Viv? You could simply be enjoying another cruise."

Viv leaned forward, elbows on knees, as she clasped her cup tightly. "I thought solving a mystery would be fun," she confessed. "An adventure beyond just another cruise—something more than lazing at the pool or having sunscreen rubbed into my back by some handsome bachelor." Her gaze drifted off as if remembering all those past cruises. She looked back at Gemma, her green eyes serious. "I've spent my adult life being seen as just a dumb blonde—arm candy for my husbands. Maybe there is still lasting love for me, but in the meantime, this 'little project' was more fun and intellectual stimulus than I've ever had on one of these cruises because I was doing it with a friend."

Gemma felt a warmth spread through her chest at Viv's words—a warmth that had nothing to do with the tea or Buddy's presence at her feet.

"What about you?" Viv interrupted her thoughts. "Why aren't you just cruising? You don't have to solve this mystery if you don't want to, especially now that it's become this serious."

"I came here to retire," Gemma sat back as she reflected. "To finally stop working all the time and start living for myself." She glanced around her well-ordered cabin, everything in its place like at Hotel LaFontaine. "I put so much into that hotel for decades…but I never really knew who I was outside its walls."

Viv nodded as Gemma continued to unravel the threads of her past.

"I was never lonely there," Gemma admitted softly, looking down into her tea as if it held answers. "I've kept myself busy all those years, too busy for anything else. Certainly too busy for holidays or friends. "

The room was silent save for the soft sounds of Buddy lapping water from his bowl and Fernando's tiny claws clicking on the floorboards as he explored every corner.

Viv reached out and touched Gemma's arm gently. "Why did you keep yourself so busy all those years?"

With a gentle hand, Gemma picked up the oval-framed photo from beside her bed—the only personal item she'd placed on display—and handed it to Viv.

"That's Tom and me."

Viv examined the photograph, noting the radiant joy between the young pair, locked in a gaze that spoke of unspoken promises and dreams just beginning. There was Gemma, the lines of time not yet etched upon her face, her eyes alight with a vibrant spark. Beside her, a dashing figure with rich dark hair, regarding her with such intense affection that it seemed to leap from the image—a smile playing at his lips.

"You married right after graduation, right?" Her voice dwindled into silence, and her eyes rested on Gemma with a mix of curiosity and compassion.

Gemma nodded. "We didn't know then how little time we had. Shortly after our first anniversary, he died. No symptoms, no warnings. The doctors told me later it was a genetic anomaly, something lurking in his DNA. It was a ticking clock we never could have heard. We had hopes and plans all sorted out. Maybe children, a little house. But in an instant, he was gone."

Gemma looked out the porthole and swallowed the lump in her throat. "I lost more than a husband that day; I lost my best friend."

Buddy nudged his nose into her palm, offering silent comfort as tears brimmed in Gemma's eyes.

"I left for London shortly after. The reminders of our life back home were too much. At least in a new city, I could find moments of respite."

Viv nodded and urged her silently to go on.

"My professional career wasn't merely about staying busy or serving others," she confessed. "I think, looking back now, I kept busy to avoid stillness—because in stillness came pain —the pain of missing him."

As she laid bare the wounds of her past—wounds that had shaped decades of solitude—Gemma realized something vital: The very thing she had been avoiding all these years was what she now found herself yearning for most—a connection deeper than polite acquaintance; something sturdy enough to lean on when waves of grief or fear threatened to pull her under.

Friendship—a word so often spoken but seldom truly understood—had taken on new meaning aboard this ship, wrapped up in murder mysteries and a vivacious blonde who wore her heart on her sequined sleeves.

"You know, Gemma," Viv began, her usually boisterous voice with a gentle murmur. "I always dreamed of true love, the kind that lights up your whole life. I thought I'd find it again and again, but it was never quite right. And here you had it—true and pure—even if only for a short while."

Gemma's heart ached with the memory as she looked down on one of the few photos she had of her beloved Tom. The pain she'd tucked away so deep it had become a whisper. Vivian envied her for having experienced something she'd chased in vain throughout her life. There was no envy in Gemma's heart, just a strangely bittersweet gratitude for what had been.

Tears mingled with laughter as they shared this moment of bonding. Vivian's flashy exterior faded away, revealing the tender soul beneath, while Gemma allowed herself to drop the walls she'd built around her heart.

"If Valentina died of natural causes," Gemma mused aloud, "no one would care about two old women—"

"Who you calling old?" Vivian interjected with a wink.

"—playing detective," Gemma continued with a smile. "But someone does care, and that means Valentina was murdered."

The realization hit them both hard. The risk was real; someone knew they were on the case, someone was worried they were getting close—close enough to make threats.

Vivian squared her shoulders, her eyes alight with determination. "I'm not just some has-been showgirl," she declared. "I'm not going to let some coward who hides behind cut-up newspaper clippings scare me off."

Gemma nodded in agreement. Her search for peace on this cruise had led her to an unexpected mission. "I came here looking for rest," she said firmly, "but I won't find any peace while a murderer is walking free among us."

Vivian placed a comforting hand on Gemma's. "I'll be your six," she promised.

Gemma tilted her head in confusion at the unfamiliar phrase.

Vivian chuckled softly. "It means I'll have your back," she explained. "In fighter pilot lingo, noon is straight ahead, and six o'clock is directly behind you."

Understanding dawned on Gemma as she met Vivian's

gaze with newfound respect. "Then let's do this together," she said firmly.

"Look," Viv released Gemma's hand and nodded toward the corner. Gemma shifted her attention and spotted Buddy and Fernando asleep beside one another, the rise and fall of their gentle breathing in sync as they slumbered peacefully.

Gemma's lips curled into a soft smile as she observed the canine companions nestled together. "Seems like we're not the only ones bonding tonight," she observed.

Their gazes met, and they exchanged smiles. Gemma sat back in her chair, a calm coming over her soul, knowing that, with a friend at her back, they could face whatever was ahead on the open sea.

CHAPTER 23

Sunlight spilled through the porthole, bathing Gemma's cabin in a warm glow. Beside her bed, the oval-framed photo of her wedding day caught the light. Gemma traced the outline of Tom's face with a fingertip, her voice soft but clear in the morning stillness.

"Tom, love," she began, her eyes lingering on their youthful faces. "I've spent far too long running from the pain of losing you. You were my best friend, my everything." A sigh escaped her as she admitted to the empty room, "I've avoided so much since you passed...how did four decades go by so quickly?"

Buddy's ears perked up at her voice, his head tilting with canine concern. "Today is a new day," Gemma murmured as she rubbed his ears, her resolve strengthening. "I'm allowing myself to feel it all—the loss and what comes after. That means friendship, even with someone as bold, bewildering, and boisterous as Viv."

Standing and stretching, Gemma dressed in sensible attire, narrating to Buddy as she did. "Only two days left before we reach The Big Apple," she mused while buttoning her blouse. "First thing's first: a spot of breakfast and then off to see Grimshaw regarding that unpleasant note."

With Buddy trotting at her side, they went through the corridors for his morning walk. The ship was waking up; the buzz of activity grew as they neared the dining hall.

Viv awaited them at a table by the window, resplendent in a teal pantsuit even at this early hour. They exchanged greetings and settled in for a quick meal. They recounted their previous night's revelations as they nibbled on fruit and sipped tea.

"I hate to say it," Gemma said with a hint of reluctance, "but I believe we must report that note to security."

Viv's face contorted with displeasure, yet she gave a resolute nod. "Let's bite the bullet—dealing with Grimshaw is enough to turn one's stomach. But once we're done, how about we lounge by the pool? Might as well give our bodies a break while our brains wrestle with this mystery."

Gemma nodded, and they headed to the lower level of the ship, where Grimshaw took their report with a grunt and snatched the note from Gemma's hand without so much as a thank you.

Feeling lighter, having discharged their duty, they quickly changed into swimwear—Gemma opting for her one-piece with a skirt and cotton blouse and Viv in a hot pink two-piece—and met again to go to the pool.

Buddy sprawled contentedly at Gemma's feet as they found shade under an umbrella by the poolside. At the same time, Fernando strutted around in his ludicrous doggy outfit —a tiny lifeguard vest with sunglasses perched atop his head.

"Never will I ever," she whispered to Buddy as she chuckled at Fernando's getup, wondering how Viv found such ridiculous canine couture.

Viv elbowed Gemma gently, tilting her head toward a tall, sun-kissed figure cutting through the water with the grace of an Olympic swimmer. "That's Alex," she murmured, her eyes twinkling with playful intent. "My favorite bartender in a Speedo is a view that rivals the horizon."

When Alex finished his swim and climbed out of the pool, Viv called out to him with an air of casual flirtation. With a confident stride, he approached, flashing a charming grin at the pair. He ran a towel through his glistening jet-black hair, lightly flecked with distinguished silver near his temples.

"Hey Viv," he greeted her with a lopsided grin and twinkle in his dark chocolate eyes. "How's my favorite showgirl?"

Viv laughed as a blush crept over her cheeks. "Better now that you're here, handsome. It's been a crazy couple of days since our lovely nighttime walk."

"I've missed seeing you down at the bar," Alex wiped a thumb over his full lips as his eyes lingered on Viv's long legs. "I'm on shift in a few hours. Why don't you come by later?"

"Consider it a date."

Gemma's eyes rolled in mild exasperation at the syrupy exchange, her mind pondering whether afternoons by the pool would dissolve into a parade of such flirtations, sidelining the real purpose of their poolside leisure.

"Shall we continue working on our little project?" Gemma asked dryly.

"Sure, hon," Viv replied. "Maybe Alex can give us a hand?"

"Hey, I've got some time before work; what's the project?"

"How about you give me two hands, and we'll tell you all about it," Viv gave a playful pout. "My shoulders are just killing me."

Alex winked, and Viv rolled over, giving Gemma a saucy smile as Alex's strong hands began to massage Viv's back.

Basking in the sun's warmth, Viv stretched contentedly across her lounge chair, a smirk playing on her lips as Alex's skilled fingers worked the tension from her shoulders.

Gemma, ever the pragmatist, seized the opportunity to brief Alex on the investigation's latest developments. Alex listened as Gemma detailed the absence of forced entry or visible wounds on Valentina's body and no apparent signs of poisoning.

"It's a real head-scratcher," Gemma admitted with a tinge of frustration coloring her voice. "We've narrowed it down to a few likely remaining culprits—Dirk, Lucia, and Henri each have reasons for wanting Valentina out of the picture. But we're missing that critical evidence that conclusively ties any of them to her demise."

Alex nodded as he worked on Viv's shoulders. "Tough case," he acknowledged. "Are Piper and Meg cleared, then?"

Gemma affirmed with a nod of her own.

Viv sighed into her folded arms. "It feels like we're chasing our tails here," she said with a slight moan as Alex kneaded out a particularly stubborn knot.

Gemma's brow furrowed as she gazed at the pool, mesmerized by the sparkles of white light that played over the rippling azure water. They had pieces of this grim puzzle scattered before them—a threatening note now included—but no clear picture was emerging.

"Have we missed something crucial?" Gemma pondered aloud as Fernando barked playfully at Buddy's reflection in the water. "Or have we misinterpreted what we've already learned?"

The frustration hung between them like humidity—thick and unshakable—as they considered their next move under the relentless sun.

The moment of contemplation was short-lived. The Captain strode into the pool area, the sharp lines of his pristine uniform accentuating his authoritative air. A genial smile flirted with the corners of his mouth.

"Ladies," he greeted with a pleasant nod. "We're making

excellent headway. The wind's been in our sails—so to speak—and we'll be docking in New York by late on day six rather than early morning on day seven. Of course, guests are welcome to extend their stay onboard if this doesn't align with their travel plans."

Vivian beamed at him. "Well, now, that's a fine turn of events! I'll be hitting Fifth Avenue for some new outfits for Fernando and me before boarding the next Princess cruise. This has been quite a cruise so far, Captain Pierce. It's one for the books, that's for sure."

Gemma mulled over her options silently. Her London flat beckoned like a distant memory, yet the allure of unknown ports whispered promises of new adventures. Was she ready to commit to a year of adventures on the Princess of the Sea? She could embark upon other ships in the Royal Cruise Lines if she wished. Or she could return to her predictable home and never know what was beyond the horizon again.

Captain Scott turned to Gemma. "And you, Mrs. Becker? What are your plans from New York?"

Gemma hesitated for a moment before answering. "I'm considering my options," she replied with practiced poise. The Captain nodded and excused himself to attend to his duties.

Gemma's gaze followed him until he was out of sight. Her thoughts churned with an urgency mirrored by the ocean waves—time was running out, with only a day and a half left on their journey.

Roused from her thoughts by an approaching figure, Gemma's eyes narrowed on Dirk Straggler. The man stood out near the pool, his typically immaculate suit now rumpled and betraying signs of duress. Muscles knotted in his jaw, and he barked sharp, inaudible words into his cell phone. With a sudden, vehement motion, he ended the conversation, the device disappearing into his pocket as his scowl deepened.

Nina approached Dirk; concern etched across her features. She reached out, her hand drawing soothing circles on his back. Gemma observed their interaction from behind her sunglasses and wondered if there was more to this relationship than met the eye.

Alex finished massaging Viv's back. "So," he began casually, laying back on the lounger beside Viv, "any idea how Valentina died?"

Viv replied with a sigh. "That's just it—we don't know for certain."

"Natural causes seem unlikely." Gemma recounted their ominous warning received just yesterday—a note that implied they were closing in on dangerous truths. "Someone doesn't want us investigating."

"Interesting," Alex mused aloud. "You know, now that we're talking about it, Henri was down at the bar drowning his sorrows in Whiskey Sours after Valentina's performance on the first night. I had to cut him off around midnight because he was having a hard time staying on his stool."

"Henri told us he went straight back to his room after the performance," Gemma remarked. "He didn't mention drinking away his sorrows in the bar first."

"Grimshaw saw him stumbling toward Valentina's cabin on security footage," Viv added. "Which adds up if he was drunk as a skunk. It doesn't prove or disprove whether he killed her with a gift of poisoned wine or any other means, though."

Gemma leaned forward, interlacing her fingers as she pondered this new information.

Alex continued earnestly, "Henri has been my shipmate for months now—and he has been going on and on at the bar over not meeting Valentina properly." He shook his head slightly. "When I returned to our room around 3 am, after our delightful walk under the stars, Henri was snoring away in his bed. The next day, when he found out, he seemed genuinely heartbroken about her death. He was crazy about her but not crazy enough to kill. That's my two cents anyway."

Viv arched an eyebrow at this revelation while Gemma absorbed it quietly.

"Could a drunken sommelier have orchestrated Valentina's demise?" Viv mused aloud, though more to herself than expecting an answer.

"It doesn't fully exonerate him," Gemma pointed out cautiously but acknowledged that Henri's placement on their suspect list had shifted down several notches.

The dead end loomed large before them—a labyrinthine puzzle that refused to yield its final piece despite their relentless pursuit.

As Gemma watched Dirk and Nina engage in hushed conversation across the pool deck, she knew they needed a fast breakthrough if they were to unravel this tangled web before New York's skyline rose upon the horizon and sealed their window of opportunity shut forever.

CHAPTER 24

*G*emma's gaze drifted from Dirk's intense exchange with Nina to the rolling sea beyond the pool's edge. A low rumble of hunger in her stomach reminded her that it was time to eat.

"See you later, Viv," Alex said, his voice resonating deeply. "Maybe we can squeeze in another midnight stroll before we reach port?"

"Count on it, sailor," Viv responded, a playful glint in her eye as she blew a kiss at him.

Alex acknowledged the pair casually before departing, his stride confident. Viv's gaze lingered on his retreating figure, her eyes drinking in every ripple of muscle beneath sun-kissed skin.

Yawning and stretching her arms above her head, Viv did not attempt to conceal her contentment. "I tell you, the man's hands are pure magic. They can soothe the worst knots—and they sure do stoke the hunger. How about we head to the snack bar for something yummy?"

Together, they strolled to the poolside snack counter, where Gemma skimmed over the American-inspired menu.

It was a far cry from her usual midday fare of soup with water crackers. Looking at the menu, her stomach grumbled as she sighed at the options.

"What on Earth is a Cobb salad?" Gemma grumbled, her brow furrowing as she scrutinized the unfamiliar item on the menu.

"Oh, hon, it's the best," Viv replied with a wink. "You've got your ham, cheese, heaps of fresh greens, plump cherry tomatoes, and the dressing is divine. It sounds so good. I'll get one, too."

With a hesitant nod, Gemma signaled the server and ordered two, though her expression remained dubious.

With plates in hand, they found a shaded table. Viv dug into her food with gusto while Gemma picked at her salad, her mind churning like the waves below. The sun bore down relentlessly, and she felt its weight on her shoulders as much as she did their stalled inquiry.

"I think I've had enough sun," Gemma muttered after a few bites, feeling discombobulated and weary from frustration.

Viv looked up, concern knitting her brows. "You alright?"

"I'm just tired, that's all," Gemma replied, rising from the table. "I'm going to lie down for a bit. I don't want my...I don't want to get dizzy by the pool, that's for certain."

Viv reached out and squeezed Gemma's hand reassuringly. "Take care of yourself. I'll check in on you in a bit, okay?"

Gemma nodded absent-mindedly. With Buddy trotting alongside her, she made her way back to her cabin's sanctuary.

On the way to her retreat, Meg appeared with an effusive smile and hurried steps. "Mrs. Becker! I just wanted to thank you again for everything."

Gemma offered a nod of acknowledgment. "It was the right thing to do."

"If there's anything I can do to help find out what happened..." Meg trailed off earnestly.

"That's kind of you," Gemma replied. She noted Meg's genuine willingness to assist but knew the complexities of their endeavor.

Meg reached into her pocket and pulled out a slip of paper. "Here's my cell number—"

Gemma held up a hand. "I don't have one of those mobile telephones."

Meg blinked in surprise but quickly recovered. "Oh, right...old-fashioned ways have their charm."

"Indeed," Gemma said firmly. "Dependence on gadgetry these days is quite alarming."

"There is a ship phone in your room," Meg pointed out helpfully.

"That will do," Gemma nodded approvingly.

Meg scribbled down another number and handed it over. "This is my direct number—ring me anytime if you need hospitality or someone to talk to."

Gemma pocketed the number and thanked Meg before continuing toward cabin 6079 with Buddy pacing at her heels.

Stepping into the room, Gemma released a weary sigh, a sound that echoed the burdens of their sleuthing—a puzzle just out of reach. She kicked off her shoes and stretched out on the bed, her limbs heavy with fatigue. Buddy, ever the faithful shadow, curled up beside her. The cabin's chilled air wrapped around them, starkly contrasting the muddle of thoughts that swirled restlessly in her head. With eyes shut, she sought respite, but peace eluded her. Visions of potential culprits, interlaced with their conjectured reasons, stubbornly pranced behind her closed eyes, mocking her with their relentless obscurity.

Sensing her disquiet, Buddy nestled closer, his warmth a small comfort against the growing chill of the air-conditioned room.

She glanced at the dog, his brown eyes pooling with concern in his black and brown face. "Meg's been nothing short of exceptional," Gemma confessed aloud to her companion. "It's rare to find such dedication these days. I should know." She pondered the idea of commendation. "I think I'll write a letter to her superior. It's only proper."

Buddy's ears perked up at the sound of her voice. He watched her intently, head tilted as if considering her words.

She went on, her tone lightening. "And I'll skip the nitpicking over housekeeping issues like the toilet paper not being crisply folded into that precise triangle each morning," she mused, a gentle laugh escaping her, "and those persistent fingerprints I spot on the dining room windows. I'll address those concerns on a different note, one that won't cast a shadow on Meg's exceptional service."

Gemma grunted and reached for the ship stationery she'd spotted in the desk drawer earlier. She pulled out a crisp sheet and a pen and settled back against the pillows to compose her thoughts.

As she wrote, commending Meg's helpfulness and professionalism, she felt a satisfying sense of doing right by someone who deserved recognition. The pen scratched across the paper in Gemma's meticulous hand, every word measured and sincere.

The letter completed, she placed it on the bedside table and lay back down, willing herself to relax. Her mind buzzed with conflicting emotions—pride in aiding Meg's career and anxiety over their dwindling time to solve Valentina's murder.

Sleep eluded her as she tossed from side to side, seeking a comfortable position that might coax her body into restfulness. Yet every shift seemed to amplify the subtle sway of the ship beneath them, further unsettling her.

"I want to find the truth," she whispered into the semi-darkness, "but not at such a cost." Gemma closed her eyes as her vertigo threatened at the edge of her consciousness like an unwelcome guest.

With determination, Gemma focused on deep breaths that filled her lungs and then left slowly through pursed lips —a technique she'd learned long ago to combat these bouts of dizziness. Each exhalation was a silent plea for reprieve from both vertigo and mental strain.

Gemma tossed and turned, searching for the breakthrough they needed as the mystery aboard Princess of the Sea remained unsolved and time steadily ticked away toward New York's shores. Finally, an uneasy sleep overtook her.

Time ceased to exist as Gemma drifted into the liminal space between wakefulness and dreams. Vague silhouettes danced at the edges of her vision in a dreamlike tableau— shadowy forms beckoning for retribution; others reveled in the chaos, their laughter slicing through the fog with sinister glee. From the depths of her subconscious arose a chilling vision: Viv's lifeless form sinking into the ocean's abyss, entwined with seaweed, asleep forever with the fish below. This haunting image taunted Gemma, a grim parody of the ominous warning left to unnerve them.

Buddy's sharp and insistent bark pierced through the veil of sleep like an alarm bell. Gemma woke with a jolt that sent a wave of nausea crashing over her.

She sat up too quickly, clutching at the bedpost as the room spun wildly around her. Buddy continued his barking, snuffling at the door in earnest.

"Buddy," Gemma gasped, trying to command room and dog into stillness.

The barking didn't cease; if anything, it grew more frantic with each passing second.

What could he be sensing? Was there someone outside? Or was it merely another passenger strolling by their door? He'd never behaved this way before.

Pushing aside dizziness and disorientation with the sheer force of will, Gemma shuffled towards Buddy with careful steps. She reached for him just as another bark erupted from his throat—one that seemed laced with urgency rather than aggression.

Gemma pressed an ear against the cool metal door. There was no sound from beyond it except for Buddy's low-level whine. Whatever had set him off was not making itself known through noise or movement.

Still unsteady on her feet but driven by protective instincts honed over the years looking out for her maids as a head housekeeper—when every unexpected event required investigation—Gemma decided action was necessary.

She steadied herself with one hand against the wall and reached for the door handle.

CHAPTER 25

*G*emma's pulse hammered against her neck as she clutched the doorknob, her knuckles whitening. With a deep, steadying breath, she twisted the knob and thrust the door wide, her emotions a tangle of trepidation and vexation.

"Who's there?" she demanded, her voice slicing through the stillness of the corridor, only to have the echo mock her solitude. "Meg? Viv?" She strained her ears, but the hush remained unbroken, amplifying her unease.

Ever the faithful companion, Buddy nudged his nose against something on the floor just outside their cabin. Gemma squinted down at a pastel-colored and innocuous gift bag. White tissue paper cheerily peeked out the top. Her cane tapped against it with measured distrust.

"What in the world..." Her whisper barely stirred the air, her gaze darting in search of Meg's comforting presence or to catch the lilt of her light-hearted voice with an explanation that would cut through the oppressive quiet. Yet the silence was steadfast in its company.

The idea that Meg might have left a thank-you gift

crossed her mind. It was a sweet thought but unnecessary. Then again, it could be another of those complimentary invitations from the cruise line—they seemed intent on dragging her to every event on board. Gemma hoped against hope it wasn't an invitation to more vocal lessons or exercise classes; she had endured quite enough of those for a lifetime, let alone a single cruise.

Or—and this thought made her cheeks burn hot—could it be from some secret admirer? The very notion was preposterous! The audacity of someone boldly leaving a gift on her doorstep on the penultimate night of the cruise was both embarrassing and maddening.

Gemma exhaled a sharp puff of annoyance mingled with an undercurrent of curiosity that stubbornly lingered. Grasping the bag, she cast a quick, covert glance along the deserted corridor's length before whisking herself back into the sanctuary of her stateroom. Buddy padded after her, his tail wagging with a keen interest, echoing his owner's unspoken questions.

"Is this what had you all in a tizzy?" Gemma chided Buddy affectionately as her heart rate lowered. "Have a care for my nerves, dear boy. My heart isn't as young as it once was."

Secure in the quiet cabin, Gemma placed the bag on her desk and peered inside its depths. A small jar lay nestled among tissue paper—quaintly wrapped with a ribbon tied into a bow. The handmade label declared 'A Treat For U' in a looping script that seemed at odds with the blatant misspelling.

Gemma arched an eyebrow at the jar's label, its carefree disregard for proper grammar both irksome and endearing. Her curiosity piqued; she wondered about the contents and the sender's identity, which remained a mystery.

Gemma deftly loosened the ribbon's knot and unscrewed

the lid, bringing the jar nearer for a tentative sniff. The scent hit her immediately: lavender laced with vanilla. Her nose crinkled involuntarily; who would dare to mix such scents? Lavender stood regal on its own—it reminded her of home, of fields awash with purple blooms under England's temperate sun. And vanilla? It belonged in cakes and cookies, not mingling with floral notes like an unwanted intruder.

She was about to screw the cap back on when realization dawned upon her like a cold wave—she'd smelled this before. Not just anywhere but in Valentina DeLuca's cabin; that distinct blend had wafted through the air amidst the chaos of discovering the opera singer's demise.

Her thoughts halted abruptly as a chill skittered down her spine. Hastily placing the jar back into its paper nest within the bag, Gemma made for the sink. With hands that trembled more than she cared to admit, she scrubbed them clean once, then again for good measure.

Water splashed over porcelain as Gemma rinsed away soap suds and traces of lavender and vanilla from her skin, trying desperately to cleanse away more than just scent. She gripped the edge of the sink until her knuckles whitened, grounding herself against the surge of implications threatening to overwhelm her resolve.

The soft whine that escaped Buddy, huddled by the door, was a testament to his keen sense of his owner's turmoil. His soulful brown eyes fixed on Gemma; he tilted his head, embodying concern and loyalty.

"It's alright," she reassured herself in a hushed tone, more than Buddy while patting her hands dry with a towel. "It's going to be alright."

Unassuming in its appearance, the gift bag remained where it had been abandoned. Gemma regarded it with suspicion and caution as if it might spring forth with new secrets or dangers at any moment.

Her hands were still damp from the rushed wash. Her heart thudded against her ribs, an insistent drumbeat echoing the dread swelling within her. No, she didn't believe in coincidences, not with stakes this high.

Gemma was near certain now—she knew how Valentina had met her end. Someone had just tried to silence her with the same method. Her nightmare, which seemed years away now, came back with sudden sickening clarity: Viv descending slowly into the depths of the ocean to sleep forever.

Viv!

If Gemma received this gift of death, then she—

"Who do I call first?" she whispered in a choked voice. "God help me, every second counts, and I might already be too late."

Her thoughts reeled, desperate for a plan. Despite his brusqueness, Grimshaw helmed the ship's security force— undeniably the sensible call. Yet, the tick of the clock was deafening, urging haste. Viv was alone, possibly in danger. She had to secure her friend's safety. She snatched the room phone with trembling hands, pressing zero with so much force it cracked her nail.

The line crackled, then smoothed out as a polite voice on the other end offered ship assistance. "Vivian Carlisle's room, immediately, please," Gemma's voice was more steel than she felt.

"Certainly, one moment, please," the operator chimed.

Gemma held her breath as the phone clicked and began ringing. She started counting down the rings to steady herself and push away the bile rising in her throat as thoughts threatened to overwhelm her. What if she was too late? Had they been utter fools to continue despite yester- day's warning? She'd only just made a real friend for the first time in decades, and now was she about to bury her too?

After an agonizing number of rings, the call connected, "Vivian Carlisle's room. To what do I owe the pleasure?"

Relief washed over Gemma for a brief moment before urgency clawed it back. "Viv," she started, her voice tight with barely contained panic, "have you received any gifts today?"

Viv's laughter tinkled through the receiver. "Gemma? Is that you, hon? Which gift?" she jested lightly. "I get gifts from fans and admirers all the time. Maybe a bartender or two, of course."

Gemma's patience snapped like a brittle twig underfoot. "This is serious, Viv," she said sharply. "A small bag containing a jar of cream labeled 'A Treat For U.' Have you received anything like that?"

Confusion and fear laced Viv's response, "Gemma, what is going on?"

"Listen to me very carefully," Gemma instructed with an authoritative tone she hadn't used since her head housekeeper days. "Do not open any gifts you've received. Don't touch anything new that's come into your room today! I need you to stay put—I'm coming over as fast as I can."

She didn't wait for a reply; Gemma hung up, grabbed the gift bag, and snatched her cane from where it leaned against the wall. She had no time to lose.

CHAPTER 26

*G*emma's mind raced as she maneuvered through the corridor at a pace that defied her usual cautious gait, with vertigo threatening at every step. The cream—the scent of lavender tainted with vanilla—had been there in Valentina's cabin on that fateful morning. Now, it had come directly to her door, and possibly Viv's.

Buddy trailed behind her, sensing his owner's distress but unsure how to assist. His nails clicked on the polished floor as he kept pace.

She reached Viv's door and hammered on it with a sense of desperation she hadn't known she possessed. The door swung open to reveal Viv's hair in a messy bun and her face half made up—unharmed but visibly startled by Gemma's appearance.

"Gemma! What on Earth—"

"There isn't time," Gemma interrupted breathlessly, pushing past Viv into the safety of her cabin. She scanned the room frantically for any signs of suspicious packages or gifts.

Viv closed the door and followed Gemma's gaze around her quarters with dawning apprehension.

"What is this?" Viv demanded, her voice taking on a hard edge as she realized this was no overreaction or jest.

Gemma's gaze locked onto the pastel bag, a twin to the one she'd received, perched innocently beside a vase of fresh flowers at the threshold of Viv's quarters. She jabbed a finger toward the item, then swiveled to confront her friend, inhaling sharply in a futile attempt to quell the pounding in her chest.

"When did that arrive?"

"Alex sent them two days ago; he knows I love roses, so he—"

"No—the bag," she explained as she picked up the offending item, "the scent...it was in Valentina's room—the same one I just found outside my door."

Viv shook her head in confusion at Gemma's rushed words.

"The gift bag has a jar of cream inside," Gemma steadied her breath to slow her speech as she tilted the bag, and the small black jar tumbled out. "I smelled the same scent in Valentina's room the morning Meg found her. Lavender and vanilla—that horrible match of scents is burned in my nostrils forever now."

"I've always had a fondness for vanilla," Viv confessed, her voice tinged with nostalgia.

"Of course, you would," Gemma replied with a touch of sarcasm, her eyebrow arching in disapproval.

Viv shot her a look and stuck out her tongue.

"So, you smelled the smell in Valentina's room and—?"

"And then I was awoken from my nap to this," Gemma gestured at the jar, "a bag identical to this one right outside my door. I thought it was an admirer's gesture at first." She scoffed at the absurdity. But when I opened it, the smell hit me—the same scent from Valentina's cabin."

Viv leaned against the vanity, arms folded as she

167

processed Gemma's words. "You think that cream is…what? Poison?"

Gemma nodded gravely. "Unless I'm wrong, and I rarely am, there was a small jar like this one in her room with only a trace of cream left. I thought nothing of it at the time, but now, I believe we've found the means of Valentina's murder —I would be willing to bet, and I'm not a betting woman, that this cream contains an odorless toxin that absorbs through the skin."

Viv's expression mirrored the seriousness of Gemma's revelation. Her green eyes locked with Gemma's gray ones in a silent communion that hung heavily between them.

"Sleep with the fishes," Viv muttered, recalling the note's chilling promise with a shiver. Gemma closed her eyes, remembering the dreadful dream, and she prayed it would only ever be just that.

Gemma picked up the jar using a tissue, then placed it back in its bag with deliberate care, her mind racing through their list of suspects. Could it be Dirk, driven by financial desperation? Lucia, motivated by rivalry and scorn? Or Henri, whose adoration had twisted into obsession? She was certain someone had tried to kill her and Viv, but who?

"Your murder weapon deduction is impressive, Gemma," Viv said, the gravity of their situation evident in her voice. "But what now? We're hardly equipped to test your theory."

Gemma straightened her back, steeling herself with a practical resolve. "We need expertise. Dr. Jim and Nurse Jo might not have a lab on board, but they've got medical knowledge we lack."

Viv nodded in agreement but motioned to her half-done face in the mirror. "Give me a moment to finish here. Can't go trotting around the ship looking like a half-plucked chicken."

As Viv resumed her meticulous makeup routine, she care-

fully placed a strip of fake lashes onto her eyelid. The trans-
formation was dramatic, almost theatrical. With one eye
framed by thick, fluttering lashes and the other bare, she
turned to Gemma, a mischievous twinkle in her eye.

"So, if the gift bag had been from an admirer, who would
have left it for you?" Viv asked lightheartedly.

Gemma remained near the entrance, her gaze fixed on
Viv's makeup application, equal parts intrigued and doubt-
ful. "Supposing it *was* an admirer," she scoffed dismissively,
"which I assure you it wasn't, my bet would be on someone
whose pockets run deeper than their wisdom. My days of
seeking romantic entanglements have sailed. As I've repeat-
edly expressed, Buddy's companionship is the only affection I require." She cast a brief look toward Buddy, who
had cozily nestled into a nook close to Fernando, the latter
having seemingly granted a cautious but tolerant
proximity.

Viv chuckled at Gemma's dry wit.

Gemma fiddled with the wire rims of her spectacles,
peering intently at Viv's face's reflection. "What is wrong
with your eye?" Gemma blurted out abruptly, her voice
louder than intended.

Viv laughed heartily, "Oh, Gemma! I'm just putting my
face on," she explained. "Surely you didn't think these were
my real lashes?"

Gemma's expression shifted from horror to curiosity as
Viv picked up another lash strip with her tweezers. "You
mean to tell me you glue those things to your eyelids? On
purpose?"

"Of course," Viv said with a smile. She leaned closer to the
mirror, her hands steady as she applied adhesive to the delicate band of faux lashes. "It's all part of the illusion. A little
glamour never hurt anyone."

With practiced ease, Viv positioned the lash strip along

her eyelid, holding it in place for a few seconds to ensure it adhered properly. Gemma watched in horrified fascination.

"But why would anyone want to add such...appendages to their face?" Gemma questioned, unable to look away.

Viv finished securing the second lash and sat back to appraise her handiwork. "Because, my dear Gemma," she began with a flourish, "when these lashes bat just so,"—she gave a few exaggerated winks—"they can turn a simple glance into so much more."

Gemma remained unconvinced but was silently impressed by Viv's agility and commitment to her appearance. Despite herself, she felt an inkling of admiration for Viv's unabashed embrace of all things flashy. The thought of applying mascara was foreign to her, let alone affixing synthetic lashes atop her natural ones.

As Viv finished applying her makeup with practiced strokes, she glanced at Gemma through the reflection and teased her about her plain appearance. "You know, a little color wouldn't hurt you, Gemma. Ever consider something more than chapstick?"

Gemma peered back steadfastly, opening her purse to reveal a simple tube of unscented chapstick. "I'll stick with my chapstick and unscented poison-free moisturizer, thank you very much," she retorted. "At least I know where they came from and that I will survive their application."

Vivian declared herself ready with a chuckle and a kiss blown to her reflection. They made their way to the medical bay with the suspicious creams in their gift bags, leaving the dogs sleeping in Viv's room.

Upon arrival, they were greeted by Dr. Jim's easy smile and Nurse Jo's kind eyes. The couple listened as Gemma revealed their findings and suspicions about the cream.

"It's certainly plausible," Dr. Jim acknowledged after

hearing Gemma's account of events, his brow furrowed in thought.

"We can't test it here," Nurse Jo added, reassuring Gemma with a touch on her arm. "But we'll bring it to Grimshaw to keep it safe until we reach New York."

"Thank you," Gemma breathed out, her shoulders dropping as she handed the bag containing the offending jars. "I'm glad we won't have to deal with that…man again."

Doctor Jim's lips twitched into a wry smile. "Oh, he'll be itching to talk to you tomorrow to get his precious paperwork into place," he said, the ruefulness in his voice tinged with a hint of amusement.

Leaving the medical area, Viv smiled at Gemma. "We should celebrate our double victory with a drink."

"A double victory indeed," Gemma echoed with a tinge of irony. "We've likely pinpointed the murder weapon, yet the culprit behind Valentina's demise—and our near miss—remains hidden. And who knows what desperate measures they might resort to once they discover we are still regrettably alive."

CHAPTER 27

*T*he weight of the day's revelations pressed on Gemma's shoulders like the dense fog that often blanketed the beloved English countryside of her youth. Yet Viv, as ever the beacon of irrepressible spirit, seized Gemma's hand and led her away from the precipice of fear.

Gemma let out a deep breath as she reflected on the day that almost ended in tragedy. Would it have hurt? Would she already be sleeping with the fishes if she'd enjoyed vanilla? Had Viv not delayed opening her gift, would she have met the same fate? Gemma shuddered at the thought.

"You okay?" Viv asked, a look of concern in her eyes.

"Yes and no," Gemma replied. "My body is well, but my heart is shaken. That was a close call, Viv. It was quite trying for me to pick up the phone. My imagination got the better of me, I fear."

"Completely understandable," Viv smiled warmly. "I'd miss me too if I were gone. For now, let's shake it off and celebrate the gift of being alive," Viv declared, her eyes glinting with mystery. "I've got the perfect spot in mind, but first, you must change."

She steered Gemma and Buddy back toward her cabin briskly, leaving little room for protest.

"But where are we going next?" Gemma inquired, annoyance creeping into her voice. "I've already had quite enough excitement for one day."

"You'll see. Now scoot! Don't wallow in those dark thoughts. Let's go out on the town—well, the ship. Change into something cute; we've got places to go and people to see. Chop! Chop!"

Gemma frowned at the thought. Her wardrobe didn't exactly scream 'cute.' It was sensible, like everything else in her life, until this cruise turned it all upside down. In her cabin, she skimmed through her clothes with a sigh. Finally, she settled on a simple gray knit dress that skirted just below the knee and draped a pale pink shawl over her shoulders to add a touch of color. Buddy looked up at her with his soulful brown eyes as she prepared to leave.

"Be a good boy while I'm out," she instructed him gently, patting his head before exiting.

Viv was waiting by the cabin door, tapping a high-heeled foot impatiently as she checked her appearance in the entry mirror. "Finally," she exclaimed as Gemma locked her door behind her.

Gemma rolled her eyes with playful indignation. "I believe my preparation time beats yours by a wide berth, Viv, my dear."

Viv chuckled heartily, the sound echoing down the hallway. "I'll take that as a compliment, Gemma, my dear."

Vivian strode ahead, the rhythmic tap of her stilettos resonating against the gleaming surface with each purposeful step. They weaved through the ship's corridors, a maze of luxury and secrets until they reached their destination. Before them unfolded the bar, a hub of social intrigue humming with conversation and the melodic chime of toasting drinkware—an enigmatic world now revealed to Gemma's curious eyes.

The bar's polished wooden panels, bathed in soft, ambient lighting, reminded her of the warm elegance in her former workplace. Gemma found herself captivated by the way the light danced over the array of bottles on the shelves, their contents glinting like precious gems awaiting the deft touch of the bartender's skilled hands.

The bartender, Alex, clad in a crisp white shirt that accentuated the sculpted contours of his arms, caught sight of them amidst the throng of patrons. A charming smile, seemingly tailored for esteemed visitors—or, as Gemma suspected, exclusively for Viv—broke across his face.

"Not one but two lovely ladies gracing my humble bar," he crooned, beckoning them to barstools with a prime view of the ocean sunset. Gemma lingered a moment, allowing her eyes to soak up the splendor of the sky set ablaze with orange and pink hues, reflecting off the undulating deep blue sea beyond the bar's expansive windows.

Gemma's gaze drifted upward, catching the earliest stars winking to life against the dusky veil. The contrast of the day's serene repose against the shadow of looming peril lingered in her thoughts, stirring a blend of anticipation and unease for the evening's unfolding mysteries.

"Thank you again for the lovely massage," Viv batted her eyelashes at Alex. "Your hands are...magic."

Gemma pivoted to observe Viv's lashes in action, a hand discreetly covering her smile to conceal the amusement sparked by her friend's theatrics.

"Anything for my favorite showgirl," Alex replied with an easy grin.

Settling into their seats, Gemma ordered a Shirley Temple—looking forward to a treat she only indulged in rarely—while Viv requested a Singapore Sling with an extra cherry on top. Alex prepared their drinks with practiced flair and slid them across the bar with a warm smile.

"Here's to not sleeping with the fishes today," Viv said triumphantly, raising her glass to her companion.

"Indeed," Gemma said wryly, raising her glass in turn. "Here's to gifts best left untouched."

Alex raised an eyebrow at their cryptic exchange as he wiped glasses before them. "Fishes and gifts? Should I even ask what's up?" he asked, his tone light but curious.

Viv laughed it off while Gemma offered him a patient smile. "We've had quite the day since you left us at the pool."

"Is that so?" Alex's head cocked to the side, a playful glint in his dark eyes. Alex leaned in closer, the mischievous sparkle in his eyes betraying his genuine interest. "You know, they say we bartenders are excellent listeners," he said teasingly. "So go on—I'm all ears."

As Viv animatedly recounted their discovery, he leaned in, the scent of citrus and gin mingling with his smoky cologne. Gemma sat beside her, silently sipping her Shirley Temple and observing with steel gray eyes that missed nothing.

"So, you think the cream was meant to do you in?" Alex's brow furrowed as he polished a glass.

Gemma nodded. "It's the only explanation that fits. I smelled the same scent in Valentina's cabin that day."

Viv said, "Yeah, and this whole thing proves our killer isn't exactly a brainiac."

Gemma added, "Not the sharpest tool in the woodshed, indeed. There was no guarantee either of us would've used the cream simultaneously. I reckon it reeks of mild desperation if I say so myself."

Alex shook his head. "So you've got the how but not the who or why. And with one day left..."

Viv's gaze turned steely. "Exactly. We make land

tomorrow night. The murderer could just walk away once we reach the land of the free and the home of the brave."

The gravity of their situation settled over the trio like a shroud. Gemma felt a gnawing urgency; they were so close and yet so far.

"You two going to see Lucia sing tonight?" Alex asked.

Viv scoffed. "Please, after her singing class and two opera shows already—I've had my fill of opera for a lifetime on this trip."

Gemma merely shook her head and sipped her bubbly drink.

As laughter and chatter swelled around them with passengers making merry on their penultimate night at sea, Gemma raced with thoughts of murder methods and motives until a thought emerged that struck her like a lightning bolt.

"Viv," she hissed, her grip on her companion's arm betraying her rising panic. "We've blundered!"

Viv's eyes widened. "Blundered? What? How?"

Gemma's voice dropped to a whisper, urgency lacing each word. "The creams, Viv. Handing them over was a grave error. Now, we may have ruined our only chance."

CHAPTER 28

*G*emma's mind raced, her thoughts colliding with the raucous backdrop of the bar. The revelation hit her with the force of a rogue wave, causing her heart to skip a beat. She turned to Viv, her eyes wide with urgency.

"We had it, Viv. The very thing we needed to sniff out our lead," Gemma said, lowering her voice to a conspiratorial whisper. "The dogs could have identified the scent and linked it to someone on board. But we turned over the cream, and now we've lost our only chance…"

Viv's gaze sharpened, a glint of understanding flashing across her face. "Do you think security would hand it over if we asked nicely?"

Gemma's head moved side to side, a slight frown creasing her brow. "Not a chance. Grimshaw would have our heads. He'd sooner ban us for life from the cruise line than help us, especially if he caught wind of how deep we're in this."

Viv frowned, her usually vibrant demeanor dimmed by frustration. "So, this case has gone to the dogs, then?"

"It's more like it *didn't* go to the dogs when it should have." With a sigh, Gemma leaned back in her chair. "So, we have something Grimshaw doesn't, but he has something we don't."

Viv arched an eyebrow, "What could that possibly be? Brains? Tact? Or perhaps a pack of breath mints?"

Gemma's chuckle, brief and sardonic, broke through the tense air. She opened her mouth to retort when Grimshaw's imposing figure cast a shadow across their table. His presence was as subtle as a foghorn, interrupting the moment with the oppressive weight of his authority.

"Mrs. Becker, Ms. Carlisle," Grimshaw grunted, his voice as gruff as sandpaper. "Tomorrow morning, my office. I expect you to provide official statements for the investigation." His gaze bore into them with the intensity of a drill sergeant sizing up recruits. "And I trust you two have learned by now to mind your own business."

"Funny," Gemma quipped, the pause giving weight to her words, "that was the same message on that menacing note."

A hint of crimson crept into Grimshaw's cheeks, betraying his annoyance as he shuffled from one foot to another. "Well, whoever sent that message had the right idea...you should leave a matter like this to professionals," he conceded, though his tone was edged with disapproval. Grimshaw's voice hardened. "Still, threats against my guests go too far. It's one thing to warn someone off, quite another to threaten or intimidate them outright. This isn't just about protocol—it's about safety."

Gemma caught Viv's eye, momentarily taken aback by the uncharacteristic note of worry that had crept into Grimshaw's gruff tone.

In the fleeting silence, Gemma's mind raced. Grimshaw's guard, momentarily lowered, opened a window of opportunity. She recalled a slip of his tongue in a previous conversation about Henri, revealing more than intended. Could she coax another morsel of truth from him with the right nudge?

"Mr. Grimshaw," Gemma interjected, "might I inquire where the evidence is currently being kept?"

His eyes, sharp as flint, were fixed on her. "It's safe," he assured her. "It's locked in an evidence bag in my office."

Viv shot Gemma a curious look, her green eyes alight with intrigue and calculation.

"And what of the suspects?" Gemma pressed on, seizing the opportunity to extract more information from their reluctant ally. "Has there been any progress on that front? Any imminent ship arrests we can look forward to—for our own sense of safety?"

Grimshaw's stance was as unyielding as the ship's steel hull, arms folded defensively across his protruding midsection. Gemma sat on her barstool, her posture erect, met his gaze unflinchingly, her wire-rim glasses catching the light as she sized him up. Viv's presence loomed beside her, offering silent solidarity. "That isn't something I'm just going to tell you," Grimshaw declared, his voice a mix of officiousness and finality.

"Mr. Grimshaw," she shifted tactics, infusing her words with the crisp English accent that cut through pretense as effectively as a sharpened blade, "have you unearthed any fresh leads concerning our persons of interest? Perhaps some confessions have come forth from passengers aboard that have proven helpful in eliminating possible suspects."

The security chief's balding head seemed to shine under the bar's ambient lighting as he shifted his weight. "One confession has come forth," he said briefly. "I'm sure you know who because your name came up in that confession. You'll be pleased to know Piper Vanderhall has been cleared of suspicion."

Viv leaned forward, the fabric of her flashy attire catching the light. "And what of Henri?" she inquired with that casual, friendly tone she knew so well to employ.

"Surely someone seen on camera stumbling about drunk near the victim's cabin with a gift is a person of interest, unless he too has an alibi, perhaps even from his shipmate?"

His reply slipped through the question like a deft side-step. "Henri has not been fully cleared of suspicion," he asserted, his voice flat as if to close the subject.

Not to be deterred, Viv adjusted her hair and shot Grimshaw a look that had melted many men before him. "You know, Michael," she cooed, "you work so hard taking care of all of us here on the ship, ensuring we are as safe as safety scissors. You could use a break. How about joining us for a drink? My treat."

Grimshaw's composure faltered, a hint of panic flickering in his eyes as Viv patted the seat next to her invitingly. "I—well," he stuttered, beads of sweat emerging on his brow. Gemma suppressed a sigh of exasperation, watching her flamboyant ally shift closer, her smile intensifying in bright-ness. Gemma wondered if this 'feminine wiles' approach might work with Grimshaw; they hadn't tested the theory yet.

Grimshaw teetered on the edge of capitulation for a moment, but then, with a visible effort, he bolstered his stance. Now tinged with a mock scorn, his voice cut the air sharply. "I'm working...unlike some people," he retorted, seeming to steel himself with sarcasm to ward off Viv's charms.

Her airy and untroubled laughter danced around them, unaffected by his brusque denial. "Should you have a change of heart," she said with a magnanimous wave of her hand, "we'll be over here, enjoying the evening, just two innocent unattached passengers enjoying our cruise."

Muttering under his breath about the likelihood of Viv's innocence being as genuine as a three-dollar bill, Grimshaw gave a perfunctory nod. He then spun around, his departure as sudden and decisive as his entrance.

Gemma's eyes remained fixed on the space Grimshaw had vacated, her thoughts whirling with the intensity of a detective on the brink of a breakthrough.

"Well, Viv, it was worth a go," Gemma huffed, the corners of her mouth tilting downwards in a blend of frustration and resignation. "At least we know Piper made her confession."

"True. You can't say I didn't try," Viv said, motioning to Alex for a refill with a wink. "At least some red-blooded men on this ship can appreciate a fine specimen like yours truly."

Gemma's nod was a distant afterthought. Her mental gears churned futilely to assemble the mystery's disparate elements into a coherent picture, each clue eluding her like smoke through her fingers.

"We have the dogs, Viv. They could've been our ace in sniffing out the clue to its source," she lamented, the frustration evident in her furrowed brow. "But now Grimshaw has the cream."

Viv's retort came swift, her lips curling into a sardonic grin. "Suppose we flutter our lashes at security, throw in a 'pretty please' for good measure. Would they cough up the cream and send us on our merry way?"

Gemma gave a slight chuckle, the absurdity of their predicament momentarily amusing despite the gravity. "Not a chance. The moment Grimshaw catches even a whiff of our involvement, he'll not only dismiss us but likely banish us from the cruise line for life."

Viv's response was laced with her characteristic sharp wit. "That's a great plan—that goes nowhere."

Gemma sighed, feeling the weight of time pressing down upon them. She glanced at her watch, its ticking hands mocking their dwindling window of opportunity. "And we've only got one day left."

CHAPTER 29

*S*hortly after Grimshaw made his exit, Gemma excused herself, her thoughts a maelstrom of clues and dead ends. Making her way back to her cabin, she felt the frustration clawing at her chest, an all-too-familiar sensation now accompanied the waning hours of their maritime mystery. Viv, ever the social butterfly, lingered behind to bask in the glow of attention, contemplating a moonlit stroll with Alex.

Gemma's cane echoed softly against the polished floor, a rhythmic counterpoint to the ship's subtle rock. Yet the soothing rhythms of the night and the caress of the ocean breeze failed to quell the storm of thoughts raging in her head. She reached her cabin and closed the door behind her with a soft click that seemed to echo her disappointment. Buddy greeted her with a wagging tail and an expectant look, but Gemma only offered him a half-hearted pat before preparing for bed. Her crankiness clung to her like a second skin as she lay down, pulling her into an uneasy sleep.

The first light of dawn crept through the porthole when Gemma's eyes fluttered open. A nebulous idea teased the

edge of her consciousness, as elusive as the lingering fragments of a dream. She lay still for a moment, willing it to
take shape, but it remained out of reach.

Gemma contemplated a brisk walk to clear her mind. She
quickly changed into comfortable tan slacks, a soft blouse,
and a cozy knit sweater to ward off the morning coolness.
After lacing up her sturdy walking shoes, she snatched
Buddy's leash from the hook and ventured out. The corridors of the ship were hushed, with only the faint, rhythmic
thrum of the engines accompanying them.

"Come on, Buddy, my boy," Gemma murmured. "Let's see
if we can find some peace for our weary minds. A morning
constitutional should set us right."

Ashore, the same routine might have felt monotonous,
but it was a sanctuary here on the ship's top deck. The sky's
canvas, painted with the tender strokes of dawn, coaxed
them to halt. Gemma stood still, letting the hush of the early
morning wrap around her like a shawl. Buddy, attuned to his
companion's mood, mirrored her stillness. Gemma paused
and offered a silent prayer of gratitude for the unexpected
journey life had thrust upon her. And within that tranquil
moment, she prayed for clarity and a breakthrough—for
truth, goodness, and righteousness to prevail.

As Gemma's contemplative gaze lingered on the sun's
ascent, a flurry of activity disrupted the stillness. Lucia Rossi,
flanked by Piper, Nina, and the rest of the chorus,
approached with a purposeful stride. Dirk Straggler followed
closely, his demeanor tense and authoritative.

"This is it, ladies," Lucia declared, her voice slicing
through the morning calm. "Tonight's performance is everything. You need to do everything for me—for us—to shine!"

Dirk's voice was firm, cutting through the lingering
echoes of Lucia's command. "You heard her," he reiterated,
eyes scanning the ensemble with a critical edge. "Nina, you

and the girls need to bring your A-game tonight. We're doubling on rehearsals this morning—no room for error."

Gemma observed the troupe's determined march from a shadowed alcove, noting the determination etched into Lucia's features and the imperative nature of Dirk's orders. Nina caught her eye, offering an eye roll that spoke volumes without a word. The zeal in their tone suggested an obsession with perfection, almost manic in its fervor. Gemma mused on what fueled their fervor—could it be a pure dedication to their craft or something more sinister lurking beneath the surface?

With Buddy at her side, she continued her walk along the deck, her mind whirring with thoughts and possibilities. She sensed something niggling inside her—was she close to unraveling the truth behind Valentina's untimely demise? Or was it all for naught?

On her way back to her cabin, Gemma detoured onto the deck where it all began. Soon, she found herself outside Valentina DeLuca's former quarters. Like so many others on board, the door was shut, betraying none of the tragedy and mystery within. She halted, Buddy, sitting obediently beside her as she stared at the door that had been the entry point to such a tangled web of events.

"What is it?" Gemma murmured. "What more could be done than we have done?" Something beckoned her to look closer, to think deeper. It was as if the air around Valentina's cabin hummed with unsaid words and unseen truths.

And then it hit her—a burst of inspiration so clear and sharp it was as if the pieces of an intricate puzzle had suddenly clicked into place. Her heart quickened, realizing she might have just stumbled upon the key to unlock every hidden secret.

"Come, Buddy, back to our cabin. We haven't a moment to lose!"

* * *

GEMMA RUSHED BACK to her cabin with her heart thudding against her ribcage, the early morning's revelation fueling her every step. Once inside, she rifled through the papers on her small writing desk, searching for the phone number Meg had scribbled on a piece of hotel stationery. Finding it tucked between the pages of her Father Brown paperback, she picked up the ship's phone and dialed with trembling fingers.

The line clicked and buzzed, and then Meg's chipper and alert voice filtered through. Gemma offered a silent nod of appreciation for the convenience of modern technology in other people's hands—though she herself wasn't ready to embrace it just yet.

"Meg, dear, I need you to meet me as soon as possible," Gemma said, skipping pleasantries.

"Mrs. Becker? Is everything alright?"

"There's no time to explain. Can you meet me outside Valentina's cabin post haste?"

"Valentina's cabin?" Meg replied. "Y-yes. I can be there in five minutes."

"Brilliant. Thank you, dear."

Gemma hung up before Meg could ask more questions. She contemplated calling Viv but knew that she was likely still nestled in her bed at this hour, blissfully unaware of the morning's developments.

Gemma resolved to update Viv once the urgent matter was addressed. At the moment, there wasn't a second to spare.

Clutching Buddy's leash, Gemma set off toward Valentina's cabin. She arrived first and waited anxiously until Meg appeared, wiping her hands on her crisp white hospitality skirt, her face etched with worry.

"I need a favor, dear," Gemma whispered as soon as Meg was within earshot. "It's vital we get into Valentina's room."

Meg's eyes widened. "Why? What for?"

"To get a sample of a cream—it could be what killed Valentina." Gemma glanced around to ensure their conversation remained private.

"What? Cream killed her? I don't understand."

Gemma's voice held an urgency that reflected the swift current of the ship slicing through the ocean, propelling them forward with relentless speed. "There's no time to explain," she insisted, her plea underscored by the rhythmic pulse of the engine. "I need your help to get into the room. It will only take a moment."

"But if anyone catches us—" Meg protested, her voice a mere whisper now. "I could lose my job."

Gemma met her gaze steadily. "I understand the risk. But it might catch whoever did this dreadful thing. I would not ask unless it was of the utmost importance."

Meg hesitated briefly before nodding and slipping out her master key card. "Two minutes," she said, ushering Gemma inside while taking up position by the door with Buddy at her side.

Once inside Valentina's cabin, Gemma wasted no time. She darted to the empty bed, sheet still amiss, which made her shudder. Shaking her head, she spotted the unmarked white plastic container sitting on her bedside table rather than under the bed.

Gemma noted with a mental nod of approval that the investigative team, led by the sharp-tongued Grimshaw, must have unearthed the container, yet opted not to disturb it further.

With practiced ease, she snapped on a latex glove from her purse. Pausing to look suspiciously at the small jar, she put on a second glove over the first for good measure, then dabbed a cloth kerchief into the jar, leaving a small amount remaining.

It's a small mercy I got here before Grimshaw did to confiscate some of this evidence, she reflected as she fastened the lid back on the jar and set it carefully back on the table. Or this entire plan would be for naught.

Outside, Meg's whisper cut through Gemma's focus. "Someone is coming!"

With swift movements, Gemma sealed the sample in a ziplock bag and tucked it securely into her handbag. Just as footsteps echoed down the corridor, she slipped out of Valentina's room. Clasping Buddy's leash firmly, she nodded at Meg and whispered, "Thank you."

There was no time for gratitude or farewells, Gemma thought as she hurried back to her cabin. We have a killer to catch.

CHAPTER 30

*G*emma's fingers trembled with a mix of trepidation and thrill as she entered her cabin, the sample of cream secured in her handbag. Buddy looked up at her with curious brown eyes that seemed to mirror her nervous energy.

"Well, Buddy, we've got ourselves the piece that may finish this puzzle," she muttered, patting his head. "Wouldn't it feel lovely to wrap this up with a bow before we arrive at our destination?"

After taking a moment to compose herself, she picked up the phone and dialed Viv's cabin. "Viv, it's Gemma. Breakfast. Grand Dining Hall. Bring Fernando and wear sensible shoes!"

"Seriously?" Viv complained with a long yawn. "Alex kept me up well past my bedtime."

"I am most serious," Gemma retorted dryly. "Fifteen minutes. Lashes are optional."

Viv ended the call with an audible huff. Clasping her hands, a spark of glee lit up Gemma's eyes.

"She'll thank me when she finds out what I've been up to,"

Gemma told Buddy, who wagged his tail in response. "Toodle pip, Buddy, we're off again!"

Viv met her in the dining hall, looking slightly disheveled. The weight of fatigue dimmed her usual sparkle. Her makeup was off—a stroke too much blush, lipstick just outside the lines. She slumped into the chair across from Gemma.

"Ugh," Viv groaned, stirring her coffee listlessly. "This isn't as fun anymore. We'll be in New York tonight, and our murderer will just waltz right off this ship. I feel so unaccomplished."

Gemma couldn't help but feel a surge of energy—a stark contrast to Viv's dejection. "I may have a solution for all those problems," she said, her voice uncharacteristically buoyant.

A flicker of interest sparked in Viv's eyes, momentarily overshadowing the shadows of exhaustion beneath them. "You didn't just sweet-talk Grimshaw into returning the cream, did you? Tell me he didn't just hand it over with a smile."

"No, I managed to get a sample of the cream—without security's help, thank you very much," Gemma leaned in a triumphant gleam in her eye.

A spark ignited in Viv's eyes as she leaned forward. "You sly fox! Well done! How did you do it?"

Gemma leaned back, allowing herself a rare moment of pride as she recounted her early morning escapade. "Well, it dawned on me during my walk with Buddy that we were going about this all wrong. There was another way to get some of the illustrious cream."

"How?" Viv urged, her voice tinged with newfound energy. "Grimshaw's got both of ours under lock and key."

"But they aren't the only samples on the ship," Gemma said, her eyes twinkling with mischief. "It occurred to me that

Valentina's room may not have been touched since the investigation began. The original container may still be there if security had yet to confiscate it. It was a long shot, but I had to check."

"And?" Viv leaned in closer, hanging on every word.

"I sought out Meg—bless her—for she has keys to the kingdom, so to speak." Gemma sipped her tea before continuing.

Viv chuckled softly. "Clever girl," she murmured, impressed.

"In Valentina's room, amidst all the trappings of an opera diva's arsenal," Gemma continued, "was a near-empty jar of cream—lavender and vanilla—just sitting there as if it were waiting for me."

"You didn't!" Viv exclaimed.

"I did indeed," Gemma affirmed with a nod. "I slipped on my glove—I always carry a pair for unexpected messes—and swiped the inside of the jar with a kerchief from my handbag."

Viv raised her eyebrows. "And Meg?"

"Meg was as efficient as ever. She kept watch while I worked quickly. As soon as I secured our sample, we slipped out just as some early risers began their morning strolls down the corridor."

"So now we have what we need," Viv mused aloud.

"Yes," Gemma said firmly. "And if Buddy and Fernando can catch the scent of someone aboard this ship…"

Viv finished her thought with a triumphant smile. "We've got our murderer."

Gemma leaned forward, lowering her voice despite the early hour and few passengers around them. "We'll let Buddy and Fernando take a whiff of this cream. Whoever they lead us to might be our culprit, and then we can tip off security to take it from there."

Viv straightened in her chair, a renewed sense of purpose washing over her face. "That's brilliant!"

With their plan set, they decided on their starting point— the ship's bow—and agreed to meet at the stern after letting their canine companions follow the scent trail.

"Let's not dilly-dally," Gemma said as they rose from their seats. "Time is of the essence today."

* * *

THE SCENT of the sea mingled with the chlorine from the pool as morning passengers lazed around the pool; an early aqua fit class began, and dishes clinked at the rooftop cafe.

Gemma's spirits rose as she and Viv searched from the Princess's top deck. She fingered the list of suspects in her pocket, wondering where this impulsive search would lead.

Gemma offered the baggie, bending slightly so Buddy and Fernando could catch the scent. "Alright, let's put those noses to work," she encouraged.

The two dogs, tails in a joyful motion, peered up at their owners before embarking on their olfactory mission.

"Let's split up," Viv proposed with a wave of her hand. "You take the port side; I'll take starboard. We'll regroup at the stern."

With a resolute nod, Gemma set off. She trailed behind Buddy, allowing his keen nose to lead them methodically through the ship's labyrinthine decks.

Gemma's feet ached mercilessly after an hour and a half, each step sending a jolt through her arches that were only partially dampened by her sturdy shoes. Father Brown never had these infernal frustrations to contend with. She lamented as her vertigo teased at the edges of her senses, threatening to plunge her into its disorienting spiral at any moment. She leaned heavily on her cane, grateful for its support yet resenting her dependence on it.

When Gemma and Viv met up, Viv caught the subtle shift in Gemma's posture, the slight grimace that flashed across her face with each step. "Gemma, hon, let's sit a moment. You're about as pale as the deck chairs."

Gemma straightened up, her lips pressed into a thin line. "No time for that. We're on the clock here." She met Viv's gaze with steel in her eyes. "I'll let you know if I'm truly feeling poorly."

Viv chuckled, her bangles jingling as she gave Gemma a playful nudge. "Remember, it's all fun and games until someone passes out. Then it's a party!"

Gemma couldn't help but let out a weary laugh, appreciating Viv's attempt to keep her spirits high despite the tension coiling in her stomach.

They pressed on, each taking their side of the ship, Gemma setting a slower pace as Buddy sniffed and explored every port side corner and corridor. The ship seemed to stretch on endlessly, each passageway leading to another, their hope dwindling with every turn.

They reached the aft deck where passengers were absorbed in their worlds, sunbathing or lost in books. Gemma glanced at Viv, noting the resolve mirrored in her friend's eyes.

"One final sweep," Gemma said, and Viv nodded in agreement. They'd see this through together, come what may.

The lower levels were quieter, cooler, and less inviting. They passed crew members who gave them curious glances but said nothing.

Turning a corner into yet another bland passageway, Buddy unexpectedly darted aside, his movements swift and decisive. Gemma's weariness was momentarily forgotten, replaced by a rush of alertness. She mustered her strength, urging her body upright, and hastened after her four-legged detective.

"Go on, Buddy, what is it?" she encouraged, matching her pace with his eager sniffing.

Gemma's heart pounded as she slipped past a sign reading "Restricted Area: Authorized Personnel Only." In the bowels of the Princess of Paradise, the mechanical hum and throb of the ship's engines grew louder, vibrating through the steel under her feet. She could taste the metallic tang of the ship's innards in the low lighting, a stark contrast to the sanitized luxury of its upper decks.

Buddy pressed on, his tail high and wagging with determination. Gemma followed close behind, her cane tapping rhythmically against the grated floor. "Good boy, Buddy," she murmured, her voice barely audible above the din of machinery. "Keep going."

Navigating through a labyrinth of piping and heavy-duty machinery, Gemma clutched at her cane with sweaty palms. A bead of sweat trickled down her temple, disappearing into her collar. The temperature in this part of the ship was noticeably higher, and she could feel herself growing lightheaded.

Gemma pressed on, however, steeling herself against her discomfort. "Come on, Buddy," she coaxed in a quiet voice. "Find it."

Without warning, an unexpected force shoved against her back. She stumbled forward, thrown off balance. Her cane slipped from her grasp, clattering noisily onto the metal flooring. She tried to steady herself, but it was too late.

With a gasp swallowed by the roaring engines around her, Gemma found herself plunging into darkness as a door swung shut behind her.

CHAPTER 31

*G*emma's world spun as a wave of vertigo struck with full force. Blinking, she reached out, seeking something solid to ground her swirling senses, but found only empty air. Her heart pounded, each beat echoing the throbbing in her head as she slid down and leaned into a cold wall. Breathing deeply, she closed her eyes and opened them again, though it made no difference in the pitch-black interior room. Buddy's low growl cut through the haze, followed by a soft whimper that mirrored Gemma's unease.

The door burst open, a flood of light momentarily blinding her. Gemma squinted, shielding her eyes with a trembling hand as a figure slipped inside, shutting them again into darkness. Buddy's bark pierced the gloom, a sharp note of alarm.

"Shh, it's okay," crooned a familiar voice, silken and soothing. A flashlight flicked on, casting an eerie silhouette against the walls. Gemma blinked, struggling to discern the intruder's identity in the dim lighting. As she steadied her breath, ready to demand answers, an unexpected thud by Buddy's paws interrupted her thoughts. His tail wagged in the dim glow, his nose busily exploring the flat object near him.

The beam of light shifted, and Gemma's brow furrowed as the mysterious figure came into focus.

"Fancy meeting you down here, Gemma," Nina Pavlova's silhouette emerged, illuminated by the flashlight on her phone. "I was hoping we could avoid this, but you just don't know when to quit, do you?"

Gemma's stomach roiled at the sight of the lead chorus member. Thoughts raced faster than she could connect as the implications of what had happened and what was about to happen became clear. For one desperate moment, she wished for a trained police dog by her side rather than sweet, trusting Buddy—who was nosing the object Nina had thrown to him with naïve eagerness—a raw steak.

"Nina," Gemma said, steadying her voice as best she could. She willed herself to sit upright despite the room tilting around her.

Nina stepped forward into the dim circle cast by her phone light. "I didn't want to do this," she began, the remorse in her voice clashing with the coldness in her eyes. "Not to you anyway; you seem alright. But for the love of everything holy, you couldn't mind your own business, could you?"

Gemma's gaze locked onto Nina, absorbing every line of her youthful visage, now marred by resolve. A gleam of unyielding intent shone from Nina's dark eyes while her hand emerged from the folds of her jacket, revealing the menacing silhouette of a compact revolver. Gemma knew if she had any chance of living past this day, she had to do one thing: buy time and pray to God help would come. She mustered what courage she could, pushing back against the tide of fear that threatened to declare her efforts futile. She met Nina's gaze with an intensity that matched her own.

"A woman died," she said tersely. "Whatever you plan to do now, I deserve to know why."

Upon receiving the cue, Nina's facade crumbled, revealing the venom beneath. "You weren't meant to get involved," she lamented. "But there you were, with your stupid friend and dumb dogs sniffing out more than you should. Clearly, you didn't appreciate the present I left for you. I had no choice but to take evasive maneuvers."

Gemma, her heart pounding against the confines of her chest, watched Nina with a mixture of fear and calculation. Having taken a tentative lick of the steak, Buddy began munching it in earnest. Gemma longed to shout or kick the steak out of her beloved boy's way, but one wrong move could end everything forever.

Nina paced before her, the phone beam swinging wildly as she unraveled the tale of her perfect plan. "It was all going so smoothly," she confessed with a manic gleam in her eyes. "But you and Blondie kept snooping around, asking questions instead of leaving it alone."

Gemma felt a prickly irritation at the disdain shown toward Viv, having grown surprisingly attached to her companion's unique style.

"Why did you want Valentina dead?" Gemma asked, her voice steady despite the danger that loomed. "What did she do to you?"

Nina's face twisted into a mask of contempt. "You never knew her. I did. For years, Valentina hogged the spotlight like it was hers and hers alone," she spat. "She had Dirk under some spell, treated Piper like dirt, and made us chorus girls props to boost her glory. Never a word of thanks, nothing more than harmonies, and never a chance to move one inch closer to the spotlight. She wouldn't share if her life depended on it."

"And you thought killing her would solve your problems?" Gemma pressed, keeping Nina talking.

Nina laughed hollowly. "I did us all a favor," she declared with conviction. "With Valentina gone, Dirk could finally see clearly. But instead of following my subtle suggestions, he put *Lucia* in for every night of the cruise. That brown-noser had the nerve to think *she* was being overlooked all this time. Unbelievable! She knows nothing about having to wait and wait and wait."

So, Lucia believed she had been scorned all along, Gemma mused as she leaned her head against the cool wall behind her. Waves of nausea assaulted her as she recalled the cryptic caption on Viv's signed photo. With a sigh, Gemma shook her head. The singer's fury at being overlooked was nothing compared to Nina's.

"So you murdered Valentina to step into her limelight?" Gemma inhaled sharply, masking her shock with a veneer of detached inquiry. Her heart hammered against her ribcage, yet her voice emerged steady, betraying none of the turmoil that churned within.

Nina nodded vigorously. "I told you she wouldn't share the limelight if her life depended on it. So I made sure her life did. And now, Lucia will have her turn once we reach New York." She leaned in close, caressing her gun against Gemma's weathered cheek. "I'm a patient woman."

A chill snaked along Gemma's back, the gun's cold metal leaving an eerie trace on her flesh. At her side, Buddy, having polished off the unexpected treat, nestled down with a contented exhale. He coiled into a tight circle, his body heat inching into her stiff muscles as foreboding washed over her.

"How did you do it then?" Gemma pressed, swallowing the bile rising in her throat. "You've fooled everyone until now."

Gemma watched Nina's face, a canvas of smug satisfaction, come alive in the harsh glow of the flashlight. Buddy lay at her feet, lightly snoring.

"You see, Gemma," Nina began, her voice laced with pride, "I concocted the perfect murder weapon. Valentina loved her creams—lavender and vanilla were her signature scents. So I thought, why not give her what she loves?" A twisted smile curled at the corners of Nina's lips.

As Nina detailed her meticulous plan, Gemma felt a shiver crawl up her spine. "It was easy enough to get a nice, easily absorbed toxin. My family in New York, well, let's say they have certain connections of the illegal variety. I'm sure you've heard of castor oil and probably shoved it down a few mouths in your lifetime. Ricin can be made from the pulp of castor beans—a little family secret.

"It was too easy to get the poison once I knew what I had to do," Nina boasted. "And for me, mixing it into the cream is a simple matter. Odorless and potent—a perfect combination."

Nina's casualness sent chills through Gemma's body. It was as if she were discussing a recipe for cake rather than murder.

Nina chuckled, a sound devoid of warmth. "But, Gemma, you gotta be careful with that cream," she taunted, wagging a finger mockingly. "Just a smidge is lethal," she boasted. Her laughter echoed off the walls of the cramped room, sending waves of dread coursing through Gemma.

Nina paced back and forth, her shadow casting long, ominous shapes on the wall as the flashlight in her hand bobbed with her movements. Huddled against the cold metal wall, Gemma watched Nina's agitation grow. Buddy lay sprawled at Gemma's feet, his rhythmic snores a stark contrast to the tension in the air.

"I tried to warn you," Nina sneered, "but you wouldn't take a hint." Her voice carried the bite of a New York winter.

"After Lucia's pathetic lesson, I left that note. Sleeping with the fishes—my family's favorite saying back home. It was supposed to scare you off, but you kept digging."

Gemma felt the knot in her stomach tighten as Nina's anger bubbled to the surface. Her hands gripped her cane tighter, though she knew it was no match for Nina's firearm.

Nina's laughter was bitter as she recounted her efforts to stop them. "I had no choice! You two were becoming a total pain in my rear. Once we dock in New York, I'll take care of business. But things are getting too hot on this ship."

Gemma watched Nina closely, each word laced with fury confirming what she had suspected: behind Nina's facade lay a desperate woman cornered by her actions.

"It's time to wrap this up," Nina declared, a manic glint in her eyes. She glanced down at Buddy with a flicker of something softer in her gaze. "I might not care too much about the people who get in my way," she admitted with a shrug, "but I'm not a complete monster. I'll let the dog live."

Gemma's heart raced as she watched Nina step closer, revolver raised—a silent promise of deadly intent. Buddy continued to snore, blissfully unaware of the danger his owner faced. The flashlight cast an unforgiving light on Nina's face, etching her fury in sharp relief. Gemma braced herself against the wall as Nina moved toward her menacingly, each step measured and deliberate. She had to think fast; there was no room for error now. Her eyes looked everywhere for any possibility of escape or distraction— anything that might save her from the fury of a woman scorned.

CHAPTER 32

Gemma's pulse hammered in her ears as Nina's monologue reached its crescendo. "You won't be missed until it's too late," Nina sneered, her eyes cold and calculating. "By the time we dock in New York, I'll be long gone, and you'll be just another unfortunate accident on board."

Nina slowed her steps, a gleam in her gaze betraying her anticipation.

"I won't make Valentina's mistakes. I'll shine just bright and long enough, then retire with grace—perhaps even take up cruising myself," she mused aloud, her gun steady in her hand as she advanced.

As she stepped closer, the door burst open with a force that sent it slamming against the wall. Viv stormed into the room like an avenging angel, sunlight blazing behind her, Fernando growling at her heels. The tiny Chihuahua, fierce as a Doberman, lunged at Nina's wrist. His teeth clamped down, and the gun clattered to the floor.

With sunlight catching her blonde locks, Viv surged forward, her body a whirlwind of righteous fury. With a swift, precise karate chop, she sent Nina sprawling to the ground. "How dare you," she bellowed.

Pinned down by Fernando's relentless grip on her arm, Nina looked up at Viv in disbelief as a retired showgirl and a Chihuahua had unraveled her plan.

Gemma didn't waste a moment. Pulling herself upright, she stumbled over to the engine room phone and dialed with trembling fingers. "Operator, this is urgent! Send security to the engine room immediately!" she commanded, her voice carrying the weight of their perilous situation.

As she hung up the phone, Gemma returned to survey the scene—Buddy was still out cold from the tainted steak but alive. Her heart ached for him as she knelt to check his breathing.

"Are you hurt?" Viv inquired, still panting from the exertion.

Glancing at Viv, who stood resolute over Nina, Gemma felt overwhelming gratitude. Words failed her as she looked at the woman who had gone from stranger to protector in mere days—a true friend forged under fire.

Security would arrive soon to handle Nina and unravel the full extent of her treachery. But for now, Gemma's gaze held Viv's with a silent thank you for saving her life aboard this ill-fated cruise.

As the sun descended toward the horizon, it bathed the rooftop dining space in a soothing glow, the golden hour of the cruise's final evening. Gemma and Viv found themselves seated at the café, a companionable hush enveloping them. They drank in the sky's canvas, streaked with the day's last blush, a herald of their journey's end. In the coming hours, the eastern seaboard would come into sight, the Statue of

Liberty's majestic figure standing sentinel in the bustling harbor.

As their drinks arrived, Gemma looked at Viv sideways, the softening light playing across her features. "I don't know how to thank you, Viv," she said, her voice a murmur against the backdrop of the ship's gentle hum. "You came just in time."

Viv waved a dismissive hand, her bracelets jangling. "I knew something was off when you didn't show up as planned. Either you were dog tired or in trouble."

She looked down at Fernando with an affectionate smile, slipping him a treat from her pocket. Fernando's tail whipped back and forth in a frenzy of delight, his tiny frame clad in a miniature black shirt, as he eagerly snatched the treat from Viv's fingers. "And this little guy," Viv continued, scratching behind his ears, "he might look more suited for a handbag than heroics, but his nose is as keen as any hound's."

Gemma watched Viv speak to Fernando with a warmth that belied her usual flamboyance. "You're my little wolfie, aren't you?" Viv cooed at the dog, who seemed to puff up with pride at her words.

Gemma couldn't help but smile at the turn of events. Nina was now under arrest, soon to be handed over to New York authorities after her full confession. It was a satisfying close to what had become an unexpected foray into sleuthing.

Buddy, having been thoroughly examined by Dr. Jim and Nurse Jo, was resting at Gemma's feet. His breathing was even and steady after the earlier scare. The relief that flooded her when they assured her he would be fine was immeasurable.

Her gaze wandered around the dining area, catching sight of Piper surrounded by the other chorus girls. They laughed, Piper's smile genuine, as she snapped a selfie with them. A moment later, they became a gaggle of gossiping hens, closing ranks to whisper among themselves.

"I'm sure they have much to discuss," Gemma noted. "Nina was playing them all like fools. Piper's antics were a pittance compared to hers."

Viv nodded, her brightly dyed hair catching the light. "It's a cut-throat industry," she said, applying an extra coat of deep pink lipstick. "Give me the glitz and glam of my Vegas stage over their opera any day."

Not far from them, Alex and Henri leaned over the railing, sipping glasses of wine and chatting amiably. Gemma noted Henri's relieved expression—no longer a suspect in a grim murder investigation.

Moments later, Rob and Meg meandered past leisurely, their hands only inches apart, grazing occasionally. Gemma smiled as they paused to offer a cheerful shout of congratulations, their voices carrying over the hum of excited chatter that filled the ship's bustling atmosphere.

Casting a glance away from them, she saw Captain Scott Pierce approaching them with his hands clasped behind his back and a smile on his face.

His voice held a note of gratitude as he addressed Gemma and Viv. "Mrs. Becker, Ms. Carlisle," he greeted warmly. "I hope you're both doing well after today's excitement."

"That's one way to put it," Gemma remarked, her water glass catching the light as she sipped her drink. Viv's lips curled into a knowing grin in response.

"The ever-vigilant Grimshaw sends his regards; he's busy, keeping a tight watch on Ms. Pavlova until we reach port," Captain Pierce said, his eyes glinting with a hint of mischief.

Gemma nodded, her lips pursed in understanding. She didn't need a personal thank you from the security chief. Perhaps, she wondered, this experience with mere passengers, two unlikely and mismatched retirees, might dislodge the cob from his nether regions. Perhaps not. Only time will tell.

The Captain's following words caught both women off guard. "In recognition of your bravery and assistance in solving the case," he continued, "I'd like to offer you both a seat at the captain's table for tonight's last opera performance." He smiled, but his eyes twinkled with mischief as if aware of the irony behind the invitation.

Gemma exchanged a dubious look with Viv. After everything that had unfolded, the opera was the last place either of them desired to be. Yet the offer was made with such genuine respect that declining felt discourteous.

"And," Captain Pierce added with a flourish that commanded their attention, "a complimentary cruise of your choice courtesy of Royal Cruise Lines."

Gemma's eyebrows raised as she glanced at Viv, whose mouth had dropped open in astonishment. A complimentary cruise was no small gesture, and it spoke volumes of the appreciation for their unexpected detective work.

Viv recovered first, her flamboyant persona slipping back into place like a comfortable garment. "Well, Captain," she said with a grin, "how could we say no to an offer like that?"

"Very kind of you to offer, sir," Gemma intoned. "If I may, I'd like to submit a suggestion for your consideration."

"Oh?" the Captain raised his eyebrows in curiosity.

"The current policies on staff relationships might benefit from a thoughtful review, allowing for some leniency. After all, committing to a year's tenure on such a splendid vessel without the possibility of pursuing a relationship with a worthy staff member seems overly stringent. Much like love, life is unpredictable, and I've learned that, often, we cannot know the amount of time granted to us in either."

"Duly noted," Captain Pierce's smile warmed as he touched the brim of his cap, offering a cordial nod that served as a subtle, respectful salute. "That reminds me, it has come to my attention that a certain bartender on board had to be reminded of passenger and staff interaction policies. Do be kind to the young man on future cruises, Ms. Carlisle. A woman such as yourself is quite the prize." He then pivoted gracefully, every bit the commander of his vessel, to attend to the myriad of duties awaiting him.

Gemma looked over at her companion and watched as a pink blush crept up Viv's cheeks.

"I don't know whether to die of mortification or take the compliment."

"Take the compliment," Gemma said with a smile. "You earned it. No harm, no foul."

"You're right," Viv laughed. "But I will miss my walks with Alex. I'll just have to admire the view. So, where to next, Gemma? You've got a free cruise of your choosing. Are you headed home or ready to set sail somewhere new?"

Gemma considered Viv's question as Dirk approached their table, Lucia Rossi elegantly draped on his arm. The setting sun cast a soft glow on the couple, and Dirk's expression was relieved as he addressed Gemma and Viv.

"I heard what you two did," Dirk began, his voice tinged with the weight of recent events. Dirk chuckled awkwardly, rubbing the back of his neck as he tried to articulate his gratitude. "Hallmark hasn't quite tapped into that market, have they? 'Appreciate you proving my innocence and keeping me from a cellmate named Bubba' doesn't quite roll off the tongue."

Viv chuckled, her laughter rippling through the evening air. She hoisted her cocktail skyward, the ice clinking merrily against the glass. "No thanks needed, Dirk. Just consider it all in a week's work," she quipped, her voice rich with the husky timbre of her showgirl days. "Just a couple of retirees making the most of this cruise life, right, Gemma?"

Gemma lifted her cup of Earl Grey with a knowing smile, the steam wafting a familiar, comforting scent as she acknowledged the compliment.

Lucia glanced at her watch, which glittered against her wrist. "We shouldn't dawdle, Dirk," she said, her tone light but insistent. "The show awaits, and we have only a little time."

With a nod to Gemma and Viv, they excused themselves and departed, leaving the faint scent of anticipation for the evening's performance in their wake. The sun continued its slow orange descent in the western sky, bidding farewell to another day.

Viv watched them go, a wry smile dancing on her lips. "Those two," she mused aloud, "either the worst or best thing for each other."

Gemma pondered the duo's dynamic. "If Lucia doesn't run him into the ground financially or treat him as Valentina did, they may stand a chance."

Viv laughed lightly. "Whatever happens between them, Lucia will be well taken care of. Dirk has quite the reputation for making the ladies hit the high notes, don't you know."

With a chuckle, Gemma pulled out her crumpled paper list of suspects from her handbag. She ran her finger down the names crossed out during their investigation. "Lucia had no idea she was even on our list," Gemma remarked thoughtfully. "If she had been behind it all, she likely would have gotten away with it, considering how things were progressing."

"Nina almost did," Viv added somberly. "She played it cool until desperation drove her to try and stop us permanently."

Gemma shook her head. "That was her undoing."

The conversation paused as Gemma reflected on how close they had come to danger themselves. After a moment's silence, Viv returned to her earlier question, persistent as ever. "So, hon," she pressed gently but firmly, "what is your next move?"

Gemma turned her gaze back to Viv and let out a soft sigh. "This trip didn't turn out as I thought," she mused. "I was looking for quiet. Instead, I found adventure."

Viv reached across the table, her hand briefly covering Gemma's. Her eyes shone. "I was looking for love," Viv confessed softer than usual, "and found a friend."

The tender moment hung between them, filled with the understanding of shared trials and unexpected cama-raderie.

Gemma leaned forward, her expression one of genuine curiosity as she inquired, "Where are you off to next, Viv?"

"Bahamas, baby!" Viv exclaimed, her voice a vibrant crescendo of excitement. "The Princess is headed south, and I'm ready to work on my tan, sip sweet coconut drinks, and dance the salsa under the stars."

"I'll pass on the salsa and too much sun," Gemma quipped, a wry smile breaking through her contemplative mood. "However, if I'm going on the next Princess cruise, free of charge, I must submit a recommendation to improve the tea selection in private cabins. Beyond that essential, Buddy and I will require self-defense lessons: you never know who else is on the ship!"

"I'd be happy to show you a few of my karate moves," Viv replied. "You never know when they might come in handy." Their laughter mingled with the gentle water lapping against the ship's hull.

Buddy sauntered over to Fernando, his tail wagging, and delivered a companionable lick across the Chihuahua's face. Fernando paused, his dark eyes assessing the gesture before tentatively sniffing back, seeming to weigh his response. Then, in a silent acceptance of the overture, he shifted slightly, allowing Buddy to settle next to him, a quiet truce forming in the shared space between them.

After witnessing the doggy bonding moment, the ladies raised their glasses in unison.

"To the next adventure," Gemma intoned with a twinkle in her eye. "May it be filled with good people, good food, and well-adjusted entertainers devoid of homicidal tendencies!"

The laughter that bubbled forth from both women was a symphony of joy, rich with anticipation for the journeys and mysteries awaiting them over the horizon.

THE END

Did you like this book?
Then you'll LOVE Secret Inheritance!

City girl April May inherits a lake house full of secrets. With the help of new friends and a new puppy, she discovers small-town charm and a deadly mystery. When a poisonous plant is left in her living room and another local almost dies, April has to *race against time* to discover the true culprit.

Available on Amazon or www.hazelsmithbooks.com

SNEAK PEEK

SECRET INHERITANCE

"You've got to be kidding me." April May double-checked that she was at the right address. Then she triple-checked for good measure. The lake house wasn't *exactly* what she'd been expecting. It might once have been a lavish place to live, but the old wood had long since rotted to a dark, moss-eaten brown. Even the lake behind was gray and stagnant, teeming with midges in the shadows of the woods.

It would take a lot of work, and she missed her decent-sized studio apartment in Chicago. If nothing else, she wouldn't be pestered by heavy-footed neighbors blasting music here. There was no other property on the tree-lined lane that meandered around the lake. Just this one, standing crooked on its lonesome.

Sighing, she grabbed her purse and stepped out of her car, her low heels sinking in the loamy soil and a foul, stale odor assaulting her senses. "Ugh!"

She looked down at her beloved Ralph Lauren leather loafers, and her heart sank to find them caked in mud.

"Nobody warned me about the *swamp*." She closed the door and treaded carefully onto the not-much-sturdier porch, covering her nose with her sleeve. The railings creaked beneath her hand as though telling her to turn back and go home.

"Why am I doing this again?"

It wasn't that she wasn't grateful for her new, albeit unexpected, property in the middle of Minnesota lake country. It was just that she hadn't asked for it. She hadn't even *known* the owner. The paternal side of her family had been a blank space for the entirety of her thirty-one years, and she hadn't shared so much as a conversation with the grandmother who had lived here.

She'd only learned about her death when a lawyer had turned up at her door, informing April of her inheritance. She'd felt not a twinge of sadness at the news of her grandmother's passing—awful, perhaps, but true. She couldn't miss somebody she'd never known. She hadn't even been sure that she'd wanted to make the five-hour journey to the small town of Laurel Lake to view the place for herself. Her mom had been the one to convince her that, if nothing else, she could spruce it up and sell it. The profit would keep her going long enough to find a new job in the city—hopefully one that allowed her to pursue a different side of journalism than the fashion columns she'd grown tired of.

A profit now seemed like wishful thinking. *How long will it to fix this place up for sale? How much will it cost?*

Smoothing down her car-wrinkled jeans, she hovered on the doormat. It read "welcome," but like everything around her, it was worn and torn.

"The most unwelcoming welcome mat I've ever seen."

A few faded pots dotted the rest of the porch, the dead leaves of their neglected inhabitants drooping to the floor.

She shook her head. "You're not here to water the plants, April. Just get in and get out."

Her reflection stared back at her in the window, shrouded by the darkness inside so that she looked unbearably pale despite her lingering tan from a summer spent by Lake Michigan. Her glossy, caramel highlights were made dull and lifeless in her blonde hair, doing an injustice to the haircut she'd gotten at her favorite salon last week. At least her makeup hadn't smudged; her green eyes were bright and ringed with cool-golden shadows to match the changing season.

She pursed her rosy heart-shaped lips and reminded herself who she was: a woman with a purpose.

So, the place wasn't what she expected. She'd manage. "You're not a quitter, April May," she reminded herself, words her mother had drilled into her from a young age. Words she'd needed to hear to survive the big city. Even if she *was* just about ready to quit her day job.

Straightening with determination, she went inside.

* * *

"Seriously?"

The interior was no better, brighter, or cleaner. Dust motes drifted in the dimming rays of sun streaming through the hallway. The fleur-de-lis wallpaper curled at its edges and, in some places, had been stripped away entirely. Black-and-white photographs hung on the walls like her grandmother hadn't lived a day in color. It shouldn't have been surprising, as she'd left her home to a woman she didn't know, but it made April feel hollow. How lonely her grandmother must have been.

"Thanks, Grandma," she muttered, taking in all the work needed in the hallway alone. The frayed, garish green carpet.

The damp bubbling in on the ceiling. The spider webs in the corners. It was a far cry from her modern, airy studio. April shuddered as she peeked in the next door.

The living room was just as miserable a sight, and the faint, musky perfume scent made April feel even more uneasy. She knew it was silly, but it felt wrong to be here, and she fought the urge to bite her French manicured nails when she heard a creak.

"Just the house settling," she murmured, glancing up the narrow staircase. Nothing but shadows and old picture frames stared back at her.

She continued down the hallway and nudged a door open. More watery light swung through, illuminating a rustic kitchen. She hoped there was a decent restaurant in town so that she wouldn't have to use it often, mostly because she was terrible at cooking, but also because the dust made her want to sneeze.

"*A-choo!*" Her eyes watered, and she searched for something to wipe her nose with, coming to a roll of paper towels on a brass holder. As she tugged, she eyed the cabinets of china sets covering the right wall. She'd been expecting this: evidence of wealth, even if the patterns were decades, if not centuries, out of date. An heirloom had also been mentioned in the will, a piece of jewelry passed down to the oldest woman of the next generation. Nobody told April what the jewelry might be, and now she suspected it was probably some ugly silver brooch now turned black. Hopefully, it was at least worth something. Still, curiosity got the better of her, and she opened the first cabinet, sending the teapots inside rattling.

Deciding nothing was interesting, she went to the next one, tracing her finger along the dust coating the middle shelf. A tall, three-tiered cake stand piqued her interest, painted with cuckoo birds and cherry blossoms.

"Okay. This one I might keep." She twisted the stand to take in the complete pattern—but the bottom plate seemed to snag on something. Frowning, she pulled the stand forward. A wad of brown, sealed envelopes had been shoved to the back of the shelf, a couple beginning to fall through the cracks.

April retrieved them, finding their corners bent and worn. Some of them, anyway. Others looked newer, less faded, and still smelled of the same perfume lingering in the living room. They were all addressed to "E"—Ellen, perhaps? That was the name of April's grandmother: Ellen Rowbury. Her son, April's father, who had passed away for reasons unknown sometime after he'd abandoned her and Mom, had been called Paul, so as far as she knew, there was nobody else these letters could be for.

And since the recipient was no longer here to read them...

April took the first letter from the pile and slid her fingernail beneath the seal, the uncomfortable feeling that she was being too nosy washing over her. *But don't I deserve to know more about my own family? A family who never bothered to know me until now?*

A faint earthy odor clung to the letter as she pulled it out. The handwriting was looping and jagged, penned in black ink. *Don't make me do something you'll regret. L.*

"Okay. That's not completely creepy." It was so ominous that her spine prickled with unease. Perhaps there was a reason Ellen hadn't opened them. Who was L? Were all the letters this peculiar?

She opened the next one.

I'll get back what's mine. L.

April threw down the letters, too jittery to read any more. She tried to think of a rational explanation for them, reasoning that it could mean anything—but that was the problem. She knew nothing about this family, including her recently deceased grandmother. Why had Ellen left the house to April, a relative she'd never met? Hadn't she had friends, and extended family, to put in her will instead? Someone else the old lady could saddle with this fixer upper? She might have understood the heirloom tradition, but the house would have been better left to someone else.

A sudden scraping noise left her frozen, coming from so close April could almost feel it clawing her skin. She waited, the silence suffocating for seconds, minutes. It came again, and she turned slowly to find the source.

It sounded as though it was coming from the back door.

It sounded as though somebody was trying to come inside.

Read the rest of <u>Secret Inheritance </u>now!
Available on Amazon or www.hazelsmithbooks.com

BONUS RECIPE

GOAT CHEESE STUFFED DATES
16 appetizers

This recipe is my go-to for holidays. It's simple to put together, mouth-wateringly delicious, and always a crowd-pleaser. They can be served hot or cold. Enjoy!

Ingredients
- 16 medjool dates (about 2 cups)
- 4 oz goat cheese 113 g
- ¼ cup pine nuts (optional)
- To serve: flaky sea salt, ground black pepper, extra virgin olive oil

Instructions
1) To serve hot, preheat the oven to 375 degrees F (190 C). Slice dates lengthwise on one side and remove the pit.

2) Spoon a dab of goat cheese into each date. Set cut side up on a parchment-lined baking sheet and bake for 10 minutes, or until warmed through.

3) If you'd like to garnish your dates with pine nuts, add the nuts to a small saute pan and set over medium heat. Cook until golden brown and toasted, about 5 minutes (keep a careful eye as these can burn easily).

4) Drizzle warm dates with olive oil and sprinkle with toasted pine nuts, salt, and pepper.

Not a fan of goat cheese? Dates pair well with a variety of soft cheeses, like:
- Ricotta
- Bleu cheese
- Whipped feta
- Sharp cheddar
- Or get wild with something hot or smoky!

Printed in Great Britain
by Amazon

41173536R00126